The Nancy Drew® Scrapbook

The Nancy Drew® Scrapbook

Karen Plunkett-Powell

St. Martin's Press   New York

COVERS

#1—The Secret of the Old Clock ©1930. #2—The Hidden Staircase ©1959. #7—Nancy's Mysterious Letter ©1959. #10—Password to Larkspur Lane ©1933. #17—Mystery of the Brass Bound Trunk ©1940. #18—Mystery at the Moss-Covered Mansion ©1941. #20—The Clue in the Jewel Box ©1943. #21—The Secret in the Old Attic ©1944. #41—The Clue of the Whistling Bagpipes ©1964. #100—A Secret in Time ©1991. #33—Nancy Drew Files: Danger in Disguise ©1989. Nancy Drew Cookbook ©1973.

ILLUSTRATIONS

The Nancy Drew silhouettes on the title page and page 180 are courtesy Simon & Schuster.
#1—The Secret of the Old Clock: Frontis ©1930. #4—The Mystery at Lilac Inn: Pg. 122 and endpapers ©1930. #11—The Clue of the Broken Locket: Frontis ©1934. #12—The Message in the Hollow Oak: Frontis ©1935. #13—The Mystery of the Ivory Charm: Frontis ©1936. #19—The Quest of the Missing Map: Frontis ©1942. #21—The Secret in the Old Attic: Pg. 3 ©1970. #22—The Clue in the Crumbling Wall: Frontis ©1945. #34—The Hidden Window Mystery: Pg. 29 ©1956. #36—The Secret of the Golden Pavilion: Endpapers ©1959. #53—The Sky Phantom: Pg. 3 ©1976. #41—The Clue of the Whistling Bagpipes: Pg. 96 ©1964. Nancy Drew® Activity Coloring Book: One page ©1979. #62—The Kachina Doll Mystery: Pg. 15 ©1981. #68—The Elusive Heiress: Pg. 77 ©1988.

Photo of "Nancy and Ned" by George Barkentin courtesy Mademoiselle. Copyright © 1964 (renewed 1992) by The Conde Nast Publications, Inc.

Cover of Nancy Drew and the Hardy Boys by Peggy Herz copyright © 1977 by Scholastic Magazines, Inc. Reprinted by permission of Scholastic, Inc.

Photo from "The Nancy Drew Mysteries" television series copyright © 1977 by Universal City Studios, Inc. Courtesy of MCA Publishing, a Division of MCA, Inc.

Map of River Heights from The Mystery of Nancy Drew: Girl Sleuth on the Couch by Betsy Caprio. Copyright © 1992 by Betsy Caprio. Reprinted by permission of Source Books.

Design by Maura Fadden Rosenthal

Library of Congress Cataloging-in-Publication Data
Plunkett-Powell, Karen.
　　　The Nancy Drew scrapbook / Karen Plunkett-Powell.
　　　　　p.　　cm.
　　　ISBN 0-312-09881-2
　　　1. Keene, Carolyn—Characters—Nancy Drew.　2. Detective and mystery stories, American—History and criticism.　3. Drew, Nancy (Fictitious character)　4. Girls in literature.　I. Title.
　　PS3537.T817Z8　　1993
　　813'.52—dc20

93-20792
CIP

First Edition: November 1993
10 9 8 7 6 5 4 3 2 1

All "first books" begin with a desire to express the self—to create a body of work that others can readily share and enjoy—along with a wish to leave a distinctive mark, however small, on the world. Too often, that vision seems too fleeting, clouded, or difficult to attain. This book is affectionately dedicated to those who helped make my dream a reality, especially:

.... to John W. Downs, Sr., a mentor worthy of Socrates, who created his own practical vision for "developing people to develop themselves" and then selflessly shared his mastery of the human psyche with me, teaching me what it really meant to "dare to dream."

.... to Alice Harron Orr, my literary agent and dear friend, who took my dream, found a forum for its expression, and then provided countless hours of advice and encouragement to keep me on track until it was fully expressed.

.... and to Andrea Kane, a literary star in her own right, whose grasp on her craft and whose understanding of the human heart allowed me to overcome obstacle after obstacle and, in doing so, taught me the magic of hope.

Contents

Acknowledgments

The Nancy Drew® Scrapbook, which required years of research and sleuthing, could not have been written without the help of the following people, who generously shared their knowledge, ideas, and collections. Special thanks to my primary consultants: Geoffrey S. Lapin, Dr. John T. Dizer, and Jim Lawrence. Also to Betsy Caprio, Ernie Kelly, J. T. Slavin, Victoria Broadhurst, Sue Grotyohann, Lonni Nash, John Van Meter, Nancy Roberts, Helen Woolverton, and Marge Romano.

I want to acknowledge the many knowledgeable subscribers to *The Whispered Watchword* and *Yellowback Library* and others who have provided behind-the-scenes support, including Anne Savarese, my editor, and her assistant, Laura Hodes; Mike DeBaptiste; Kate Emburg; Anita Sue Grossman; Linda Joy Singleton; Jack Santore; Gil O'Gara; and Melanie Knight.

A special acknowledgment is due to an equally special group of people who have provided peace of mind, resources, and sometimes sanctuary to allow me to finish this book: Joe and Joanne Lancellotti; "Margaret"; Nick and Elaine DeRizi; Patricia Leary; Donna and Michael Steinhorn; Jonathan Orr; Rich Leary; Clare Wharton; Becky Rosas; Kathryn Ondov-Quick; Johnnie Ryan-Evans; Wendi Kane; Brad Kane; Marie Lance. Chief Hoffman and the Rumson Police Department; Hudson County Assistant Prosecutor James Duffy, my attorney; and Vincent Verdiramo, Jr. Heartfelt thanks to my cousin and good friend Joe Lance, to my mother, Rosemarie Plunkett, to my little boy, Jason, and to the memory of Nonnie.

The Intriguing Publishing History of America's Favorite Teen Detective

Reflections of Nancy Drew: The Case of the Fourteen-Carat Sleuth

Hidden staircases and musty old attics . . . wooden statues echoing eerie chants . . . twisted candles flickering at midnight . . . blood-curdling screams and abandoned pirate ships . . . ghostly figures, cloaked in mist, stalking ancient mansions . . .

These are the images of Nancydrewland—images that have effectively thrilled youngsters for more than sixty years, keeping eight- to twelve-year-old girls under their bedcovers with flashlights, pupils dilated and hearts pounding. Contemporary mystery author Nancy Pickard spoke for many fans in her 1991 tribute "I Owe It All to Nancy Drew": "I could hardly bear to turn the page for fear of what might happen next, and yet I couldn't help turning the pages to see what happened next. Oh, it was wonderful!"

Indeed, generations of fans have wondered, while engrossed in dog-eared blue or yellow volumes, if Nancy *would ever get out of this jam alive.*

Of course she did . . . and still does. Supersleuth Nancy Drew would never let her readers or her clients down. She consistently uses her brains, talent, and sometimes a well-placed karate kick to squeak out of perilous situations and make certain all evildoers receive due comeuppance. There is never any doubt about how a Nancy Drew mystery will end, nor a variation from the familiar, comfortable-as-an-old-shoe plot structure: an intriguing, riveting opening; a summary of the current dilemma; a series of cliff-hangers; menacing warnings to stay off the case; a chase scene; a proper resolution; and a tantalizing promise of what is in store for Nancy "in the next episode."

It is a tried-and-true mystery sequence that, when combined with an admirable, attractive heroine, interesting settings, plenty of action, and a fabulous marketing campaign, has

Overleaf: Nancy Drew's first mystery was *The Secret of the Old Clock.* Applewood Books issued this facsimile edition, with an introduction by mystery novelist Sara Paretsky, in 1991. (Simon & Schuster/Applewood Books)

amounted to a winning formula. Nancy's stories, written under the pen name of Carolyn Keene and originally published in hardcover by Grosset & Dunlap, have sold over eighty million copies in more than seventeen languages, including Malay, Icelandic, and Chinese. Sales have surpassed those of her male counterparts, The Hardy Boys (started in 1927), and even those of mystery's grande dame, Agatha Christie.

Today's readers can choose from updated versions of the Grosset & Dunlap hardcover titles their parents and grandparents enjoyed, then roll along to the new paperback titles (beginning with volume #57, *The Triple Hoax*) that Simon & Schuster has produced since 1979. The Nancy Drew Files, a more sophisticated mystery/romance series, is available for young adults who have graduated from the traditional series. In 1988 Simon & Schuster also introduced the Nancy Drew & Hardy Boys SuperMystery series for preteen boys and girls seeking double-trouble adventure books. Picture books, story collections, and other spin-offs followed. All this amounts to a feast of fast-paced crime-solving fiction for young readers.

It is doubtful that even Nancy Drew's creator, the prolific optimist Edward Stratemeyer, would have predicted such runaway success from one of his 125 literary offspring. Yet Nancy's fans, critics, competitors, even her chums Bess Marvin, George Fayne, and Ned Nickerson, all realized that Nancy was special—from day one, line one.

America's blond-haired, blue-eyed, lock-picking dynamo instantly captured readers' hearts when the first title in the series, *The Secret of the Old Clock*, was released in 1930. And why not? Unlike the majority of her rather prim, Victorian predecessors, Nancy burst onto the scene early in the Great Depression as a courageous, intelligent, and inspiring heroine. With an unlimited supply of luck, this gothic Girl Scout could do anything, while her father, the illustrious Carson Drew, provided a steady stream of emotional support (and spending money) to aid her noble pursuits.

Nancy arrived ten years after American women won the right to vote—and she arrived in style, without an ounce of time wasted contemplating her gender's alleged limitations. In the preface to the facsimile reproduction of *The Bungalow Mystery* (Applewood Books, 1991), novelist P. M. Carlson stressed the importance of Nancy Drew as a positive role model for impressionable adolescent girls in the 1930s and 1940s.

Spring 1930	Grosset & Dunlap releases the first three Nancy Drew mysteries: *The Secret of the Old Clock*, *The Hidden Staircase*, and *The Bungalow Mystery*.
1932	The famous 1930s Nancy Drew silhouette, designed by Russell Tandy, is added to the covers and endpapers of volumes #1 through #8.
1937–38	Warner Brothers releases four Nancy Drew movies starring Bonita Granville.
1947	The second, 1940s version of the Nancy Drew silhouette appears on covers and endpapers.
1957	Parker Brothers issues the first and only Nancy Drew Mystery Game.
1962	The first updated and revised editions of Nancy Drew volumes #1 through #34 begin to arrive in bookstores.
1967	A Nancy Drew doll is issued by the Madame Alexander Doll Company.
1973	Grosset & Dunlap publishes *The Nancy Drew Cookbook: Clues to Good Cooking*.
1977	Premier of the "Hardy Boys/Nancy Drew Mysteries" television series on ABC.
	The first "picture book" Nancy Drew mysteries for ages five to eight are published by Grosset & Dunlap.
1979	Simon & Schuster issues the first Nancy Drew paperback mystery (volume #57, *The Triple Hoax*).
1980	Nancy Drew's fiftieth anniversary.
1981	Publication of *The Nancy Drew and the Hardy Boys Short Story Collection: Eight New Mysteries* (Simon & Schuster).
1983	The first volume of *Nancy Drew Ghost Stories* is published by Simon & Schuster. (A second volume appeared in 1985.)
1984	The Nancy Drew series *Be a Detective Mystery Stories* begins. The first volume of the Nancy Drew Files, a mystery/suspense series for young adults, is published by Simon & Schuster.
1988	The debut of *Nancy Drew & Hardy Boys SuperMystery* series (Simon & Schuster).
1989	First volumes of *River Heights USA*, a spin-off of the Nancy Drew mysteries, are published by Simon & Schuster.
1991	Publication of the one hundredth Nancy Drew mystery, *A Secret in Time*, an anniversary edition featuring the old clock from volume #1 in a brand-new story.

According to Carlson, the message in Nancy Drew mysteries was clear: "Yes, we're female, but we too can hunt down truth! We can fight for justice! We too can have adventures! We can do it!"

Girls loved the spirit of Nancy then . . . and they love her now. Although contemporary fans have grown to expect much more freedom than did their suffragette great-grandmothers, they still revel in Nancy Drew's aura of self-confidence. Decades after her birth, America's favorite sleuth remains a literary celebration of just how far a female's capabilities can take her. In a 1992 interview with the Hudson County *Jersey Journal*, Tricia Zimic, a Nancy Drew cover illustrator, phrased it well: "Nancy Drew can help young girls feel strong and powerful in their world. If Nancy is in trouble, they know she'll get out of it." The reporter, Sally Deering, added: "And now Drew is a credit-card carrying, sports-car driving, videocassette-viewing woman of the 90s." In spite of Nancy's sometimes too-perfect image, these modern qualities prompt preteens to identify with her—and to stand in line at the local library or bookstore to get the latest title in the series.

Nancy Drew exudes her characteristic confidence, daring, and thirst for adventure in this frontispiece from *The Message in the Hollow Oak*. (Simon & Schuster)

In 1990 Nancy Drew celebrated her sixtieth birthday, yet she is forever eighteen, forever valiant, forever victorious, and, of course, forever in the green. The series has reaped fourteen-carat profits for her publishers and fourteen-carat thrills for her fans.

Yet the enormous commercial success of Nancy Drew, and her current status as a household name, is not just an issue of dollars and exclamation points. What is most intriguing, even amazing, is the sheer staying power of her appeal. The Nancy Drew Mystery Stories are the best-known, longest-running girls' detective series in publishing history—bar none!

Which brings to mind a few questions.

Why did Nancy withstand the test of time when so many other heroines disappeared from bookshelves, and often from memory? How did she manage to survive the uncertain thirties, the war-racked forties, the fabulous fifties, even the pop-art sixties, without breaking stride? Readers, scholars, librarians, and booksellers have offered up theories for six decades, but the debate continues.

What single, magical ingredient makes Nancy Drew so successful?

There is no definitive answer. In her recent book *The Mystery of Nancy Drew: Girl Sleuth on the Couch*, Betsy Caprio wrote, "More than one riverbed of unconscious imagery was tapped into her by her creators—unknowingly, of course—and these channels filled up, came together, and still flow strong today."

Nancy Drew's unprecedented popularity is a product of engaging, fast-paced texts, perfect historical timing, healthy publishing economics, exceptionally strong responses from readers, and of special note, visual impact. As we'll see in chapter 4, the original Nancy Drew mysteries were beautifully illustrated by artist Russell H. Tandy, whose color dust jackets virtually leaped off the shelves in the 1930s, overshadowing the bevy of titles issued during the golden age of children's series books. The combination of riveting stories and eye-catching artwork added up to an astounding, far-reaching commercial appeal.

And let's not forget about Nancy Drew herself . . .

The Nancy of past and present radiates the type of appeal that seeps into our minds, works its way to our hearts, then ingrains itself in our souls, eventually becoming part of our daily lives. Quite frankly, she has star quality.

Nancy Drew is the Barbie of the written word, the Shirley Temple of the teen set, the Dorothy of detection, complete with her own Oz-like hometown of River Heights and her own dog named Togo. "That Drew girl" shares one elusive quality with these other fictional heroines that guarantees a best-seller: the "wish it were me" factor. Fans old and new do not simply enjoy *reading* about Nancy Drew—they dream of *being* her, even for a day.

In her analysis of the psychological appeal of Nancy Drew, Betsy Caprio even compared Nancy Drew to a goddess, a divine feminine whom young girls longed to emulate: "Just as a classical Greek drama often featured the deus ex machina, a deity lowered onto the stage to set right the lives of everyday folks, so too does a greater-than-real Nancy Drew arrive at scene after scene to set things straight for those she encounters. Nancy is a helper, like earlier virgin goddesses, [such as] brainy Athena and . . . Artemis, the champion of women."

Along with her goodness (which is often concealed behind an aloof, restrained personality), Nancy offers readers a glimpse into an enchanted life. Who wouldn't love to take part in exotic, dangerous adventures, enjoy an unlimited bank account, achieve international honor for unselfish heroism, bask in a fathomless well of love and support, and race about town in her own modern version of a roadster—a sleek blue Mustang?

MISS BILLY'S DECISION
ELEANOR H. PORTER

DONNA PARKER at CHERRYDALE

MISS PAT'S HOLIDAYS at GREYCROFT

PEMBERTON GINTHER

The GIRL SCOUTS AT BELLAIRE

✳ ✳ LILIAN GARIS ✳ ✳

Since the late 1800s, countless girls' series have come and gone, but Nancy Drew has withstood the test of time.

Although Nancy's critics often lambast this very representation of life for its unrealistic message to readers, one must also ask: Does a star like Nancy Drew deserve anything less? Should young girls, if they aspire to lofty goals, stifle their dreams?

Until now, most readers have been able to enjoy Nancy Drew and company only as pieces of a large puzzle. In 1930 Nancy materialized as a lively yet rather one-dimensional character; through the years she was fleshed out, one trait at a time, one book at a time, one cliff-hanger at a time, into a bona fide supersleuth. Today Nancy Drew has a complete résumé, a wealth of experience, and a long history to call her own. Her hometown of River Heights is now a thriving metropolis and her love life has become . . . well, spicier.

Since her debut, Nancy has also inspired four motion pictures, several plays, a ballet, a network television show, and a rock group. In April 1993, Nancy's official birthday month, the University of Iowa even hosted the first Nancy Drew conference. Nancy has been immortalized in the form of a doll, been capitalized on through games, puzzles, and lunch boxes, and become the object of fan clubs. And because her series inspires reader nostalgia, Nancy Drew has expanded into the collectibles market. Fans spanning four generations are actively amassing vintage titles, products, and memorabilia—at prices that would stun even the richest of heiresses Nancy was so adept at assisting.

So, fellow fans, it is time to become reacquainted with America's favorite teenage sleuth. As you leaf through the pages of this scrapbook, may you be filled with happy memories and begin to wonder, all over again:

> Will Nancy ever go to college? Will she ever accept payment for her work? Will she ever age? Will Carson Drew ever put a hold on Nancy's charge cards? What actually happened to Nancy's deceased mother? What is George Fayne's true given name? Will Nancy ever break down and marry Ned Nickerson? And of course, was there really a Carolyn Keene?

Perhaps, if you position your magnifying glass just so, you will find clues to these unsolved mysteries . . .

Nancy Drew: The Literary Offspring of Edward Stratemeyer

FOR decades the facts concerning Nancy Drew's birth and publishing history were obscured by folklore and half-truths. The series' original packager, the Stratemeyer Syndicate, hid Nancy Drew's author behind a pseudonym and fiercely protected its possession of the character. During the first quarter of the twentieth century, the helmsman of the operation was the prolific Edward Stratemeyer, a man as elusive as his creative offspring, Nancy Drew. Stratemeyer's penchant for secrecy reached new heights when the syndicate was passed along to his daughter, Harriet S. Adams. Between 1930 and 1982, Adams not only made publishing history but also occasionally rewrote it to suit the syndicate's publicity needs. As a result, numerous journalists and authors, through no fault of their own, have circulated misinformation about the Nancy Drew series and its author, Carolyn Keene. Even as this book is published, a large portion of the story has yet to unfold.

We can quickly dispense with one widespread myth about the Nancy Drew mysteries: Edward Stratemeyer did not actually write them. (The person who did pen those early Drews is discussed in chapter 3.) However, it is an undisputed fact that Nancy Drew was Stratemeyer's idea, and he did develop brief outlines for the first four books in the series. Further, without his keen insight and powerful business clout, The Secret of the Old Clock, The Hidden Staircase, and The Bungalow Mystery would not have become overnight sensations. To truly comprehend the formidable connection between Nancy Drew's success and that of her creator, we must travel back to a time well before her birth, to the golden age of children's series books, and examine the golden touch of its reigning king.

Edward Stratemeyer, circa 1910.

Edward Stratemeyer

The Man of a Hundred Names

Edward Stratemeyer, a prim-looking Victorian gentleman who remained a child at heart, was born on October 4, 1862, in Elizabeth, New Jersey. Like other youngsters of his generation, he enjoyed the books of Horatio Alger and Oliver Optic, along with the five- and ten-cent novels, weekly story papers, and boys' magazines then flooding the market. By the time Stratemeyer was in his twenties, fictional detective Nick Carter and western adventurer Buffalo Bill Cody were national heroes.

Much of the inexpensive fiction available to boys and girls in the latter part of the 1800s featured the daring exploits of swashbuckling heroes on the open seas, gun-slinging cowboys in the Wild West, and ambitious country lads who turned their rags into riches. Both the style of these fast-moving, escapist stories and the way they were successfully mass-marketed left a lasting impression on Stratemeyer, one he would eventually call on to alter the world of children's publishing forever.

Amazingly, four of the children's series that Stratemeyer created behind pseudonyms are still published today, in updated versions, by Simon & Schuster. The "big four" include The Bobbsey Twins (by Laura Lee Hope, begun in 1904); Tom Swift (Victor Appleton, 1910); The Hardy Boys (Franklin W. Dixon, 1927); and of course Nancy Drew (Carolyn Keene, 1930). Stratemeyer's personal favorite, the Rover Boys (by Arthur M. Winfield), also enjoyed long-term success: between 1899 and 1926 that series alone produced thirty volumes, was distributed by four different publishers, and sold more than five million copies.

Because of his penchant for pseudonyms, Edward Stratemeyer is not a household name like many of his fictional heroes and heroines. In fact, Stratemeyer wrote, edited, and published so many different stories and books under so many names that no one is exactly certain how much material he personally generated in his lifetime. At one time he even wrote under the name of *another* famous author, Horatio Alger, Jr.! After his friend died in 1899, Stratemeyer obtained legal rights to much of his work and eventually completed eleven Alger volumes, which were published by Mershan, and later Grosset & Dunlap, as part of the Horatio Alger, Jr. Rise in Life series.

It is hard to believe one person managed to do so much in such a relatively short time. But it was not a wish made on Aladdin's lamp that helped Stratemeyer turn his gift for telling tall tales into gold. It was a combination of three qualities: uncanny insight into the minds of children; acute awareness of current publishing economics; and subdued but potent charisma. He had great skill at persuading others to do his bidding, on his terms, while he reaped the lion's share of profits.

Where It All Began: Folklore Versus Fact

To this day, primarily as a result of post-1930 syndicate-generated publicity, Stratemeyer is commonly thought to have burned with a desire to be a famous writer. It has also been widely reported that Stratemeyer published his first story, "Victor Horton's Idea," in *Golden Days* magazine in Philadelphia in 1889, shortly before his marriage to Magdalene B. VanCamp. Legend has it that he wrote the original draft on brown wrapping paper while working in his half brother's tobacco store.

However, series-book collector and author Dr. John T. Dizer, who has been studying the Stratemeyer phenomenon for forty years, recently came across evidence to the contrary. In Dizer's scholarly paper *Impressions of Edward Stratemeyer*, published in March 1990, he points out that at least five items were written by Stratemeyer *before* 1889. Of these, two are especially important to note. The first is a story entitled "Harry's Trial," published in *Our American Boys* (Elizabeth, New Jersey) in January 1883 under the pen name "Ed. Ward." Another is the libretto of *Love's Maze*, a comic opera in two acts that was registered with the Library of Congress Copyright Office in 1887 by Edward and Louis Charles Stratemeyer. (Louis Charles was Edward's half brother.) It is uncertain whether the opera was ever produced, but the evidence does show that Stratemeyer's writings extended to the performing arts.

As far as Stratemeyer's alleged "burning desire" to be a writer, Dizer feels strongly that economic interest rather than artistic aspiration led Stratemeyer into the commercial fiction field: "Stratemeyer did sell some of his work while he kept the tobacco shop and 'finding writing paid' [Stratemeyer's own words], he finally went full-time into writing."

It may be true that after Stratemeyer sold "Victor Horton's Idea" for seventy-five dollars (a lot of greenbacks in 1889) he enthusiastically filled steady requests he received for more material, seeing an opportunity to make a good deal of money. But if Stratemeyer did pen the first draft of a story on brown wrapping paper, it was probably not "Victor Horton's Idea," but an earlier work.

In 1893 Stratemeyer was hired as the editor of *Good News*, a major weekly boys' story paper published by Street and Smith. Here he learned firsthand the intricacies and daily operations of the publishing business. By age thirty-five, Stratemeyer was publishing his own weekly boys' magazine, *Bright Days*. During this stage of his career, Stratemeyer worked with his own literary mentors, Alger, Optic, and Edward Ellis. He also worked with William Gilbert Patten, who was known to boys across America as Burt L. Standish, author of the best-selling "dime novel" Frank Merriwell series that debuted in 1896.

Stratemeyer's creative output between 1889 and 1904, the year he started his own literary syndicate, is legendary. He wrote more than eighty boys' serials for ten different magazines and story papers, and published one hundred books. Stratemeyer's popular Colonial series was issued in hardcover by Lee & Shepard from 1901 to 1906, and beginning in the early 1890s much of his work was being serialized, under his own name and several pseudonyms, in weekly magazines and story papers such as *Argosy*, *Holiday*, and *Golden Days*. (Somehow, he also found time to manage his own stationery store in Newark, New Jersey, from 1889 to 1896.)

Stratemeyer's story serials covered an astounding range of topics. Writing as P. T. Barnum, Jr., he created "Limber Leo, Clown and Gymnast"; as Emerson Bell, he wrote "The Electric Air and Water Wizard"; as Edward Stratemeyer he gave his readership "Jack, the Inventor: The Trials and Triumphs of a Young Machinist." He wrote paperback dime novels as Jim Bowie and Jim Daly, and women's serials as Julie Edwards. His first hardcover book, *Richard Dare's Venture* (Merriam) appeared in 1894, having been published previously as a magazine serial for *Argosy* in 1881.

In 1898 a milestone in American history provided the fuel for Stratemeyer's first official best-seller. As Commodore George Dewey and the Spanish American War were making front-page headlines, Stratemeyer dashed off *Under Dewey at Manila* (Lee & Shepard). The book sold out (it eventually went through twenty printings) and its success led to an enthusiastic demand for sequels. Stratemeyer quickly wrote five more novels, which appeared under the umbrella title The Old Glory series.

This is but one example of Stratemeyer's genius for anticipating and capitalizing on topical events. As Dizer notes in his book *Tom Swift and Company* (McFarland, 1982): "When Lindbergh flew the Atlantic in 1927 Stratemeyer had the first volume of Ted Scott, *Over the Ocean to Paris*, finished in two weeks and had it in stores in less than four." The Ted Scott series (Grosset & Dunlap) continued until 1943, released under the pseudonym of F. W. Dixon, the same pen name Stratemeyer would soon use for the Hardy Boys series.

During the heyday of the industrial revolution, Stratemeyer contrived the fiction formula that would become his hallmark. He combined the rags-to-riches themes of the late 1900s with the excitement of early-twentieth-century technology. His heroes were intelligent, resourceful, and strong, in keeping with the late-Victorian preference for characters of high moral fiber, but they also zipped around in airships and motor cars, facing dangerous international foes. Nowhere is this better illustrated than through the following summary of the adventures of Stratemeyer's science fiction brainchild, Tom Swift, in *Tom Swift and His Electric Runabout*:

Back in 1913, Edward Stratemeyer capitalized on the exciting new world of aviation in boys' series books such as *Dave Dashaway and the Young Aviator* (left). More than sixty years later his female creation, Nancy Drew, was also in the skies—skillfully piloting her way through the clouds to aid her pals in *The Sky Phantom* (1976). (Simon & Schuster)

"The girls are trying to signal me!" Nancy said. "Maybe something is wrong."

[Tom's] electric runabout was quite the fastest car on the road, and when he sent his wonderful wireless message he saved himself and others from Earthquake Island. He solved the secret of the diamond makers, and though he lost a fine balloon in the caves of ice, he soon had another air craft—a regular sky-racer. His electric rifle saved a party from the red pygmies in Elephant Land, and in his air glider he found the platinum treasure.

Is it any surprise boys found these books irresistible?

Stratemeyer did not forget his female readers, however. They were treated to the adventures of Dorothy Dale, the Motor Girls, and the memorable Ruth Fielding, who debuted in 1913 as a poor orphan, established herself as a motion picture producer, and became the Duchess of Sharlot by the time her series ended in 1934. Amid his fast-paced plots and plucky characters, Stratemeyer wove the magic of the American Dream.

Stratemeyer filled his readers with a sense of wonder and hope—something sorely needed in those trying times. In *Dave Dashaway, the Young Aviator* (1913), the hero flees from his abusive guardian to make his mark in the exciting new world of aeronautics: "It seemed to him as though at the touch of a magician's wand his whole life had been changed—as if the ardent desires of his heart had been granted. . . . Dave's eyes filled with grateful tears. He felt as if suddenly he had found his right place in life and real home."

This card from the Library of Congress, dated 1919, lists some of Edward Stratemeyer's many pseudonyms: William Taylor Adams, Arthur M. Winfield, Captain Ralph Bonehill, and Edna Winfield.

Stratemeyer's Dilemma

In *Smithsonian* magazine (October 1992), journalist Bruce Watson aptly described Stratemeyer as a man who went beyond the role of mere author into the realm of a "literary machine." This statement takes on even greater meaning when we look at the second phase of Stratemeyer's publishing career.

By age forty Stratemeyer was a great commercial success, but he faced two major problems. The first was that parents and children were having trouble coming up with the 75¢ to $1.25 needed to purchase juvenile hardcovers.

To resolve this, he proposed to Mershan and Lee & Shepard, his publishers at the time, that they sell his books for fifty cents, thereby putting them within the financial reach of the average-income family. The idea took off. Boys and girls gobbled up the attractively bound, economically priced hardcovers. Soon, other juvenile publishers followed suit, creating what could be considered a golden age of fifty-centers.

Still, Stratemeyer was not satisfied. He had to address his second problem, which was that his mind worked faster than his fingers could fly across a typewriter, and certainly they were not going fast enough to meet the growing demand for his tales. There were so many unexplored ideas he wanted to share, so much opportunity, so much pent-up creativity inside his overworked soul, that he just had to come up with a solution.

Between 1904 and 1905 he started his own literary syndicate to produce books at a faster pace.

Stratemeyer set up shop at 24 West Twenty-fifth Street in Manhattan, placed ads in the classifieds, and hired a small staff of ghostwriters. The concept of a book-packaging house was not a new idea in publishing, but Stratemeyer capitalized on it with unprecedented success. In essence, Stratemeyer would think up a book idea, write a short plot outline, and pay other writers to finish the job—usually at record speed, forty days or less. The first ghostwriters employed by the syndicate received flat fees ranging from fifty to one hundred dollars per book. In return they signed over all rights to the work and house names to the syndicate, which then sold limited print rights to established publishers. It was a remarkably lucrative setup, and even though Stratemeyer's staff was getting less than its fair share, during hard times their fifty dollars or so probably seemed like a fortune.

Stratemeyer took great pride in the work produced by his syndicate and hired writers who were, with rare exception, talented as well as fast. Several members of his free-lance staff, which included Howard Garis, Lillian Garis, Leslie McFarlane, and Mildred Wirt, were successful authors in their own right. Both the syndicate-controlled and independent titles they produced are now cherished by collectors.

The Birth of Nancy Drew

In 1927 Stratemeyer introduced what would prove to be the syndicate's most commercially successful boys' series, The Hardy Boys. By 1929 the Hardys had become so popular that Stratemeyer decided to create a female counterpart to brothers Joe and Frank. He dreamed up a character with blond hair, blue eyes, and a dashing blue roadster—a girl with pluck and good sense and a thirst for adventure, a spirited teen who would not only satisfy an unmet need, but also sell enough copies to make a moderate profit. Nancy Drew was born.

Stratemeyer prepared a one-page outline for the new girls' series and sent it off to a young midwestern author he'd worked with before. Could she come up with a sample book? She could, and she sent the completed manuscript to Stratemeyer for review. Two additional titles were written, Grosset & Dunlap was awarded print rights, and the presses started humming.

The first gray-blue Nancy Drew hardcovers, which featured colorful dust jackets, hit the stores late in March 1930—and quickly sold out.

Nancy Drew's innate appeal, combined with the powerful clout Stratemeyer wielded in the publishing industry and the talent of the ghostwriter behind the name of Carolyn Keene, had secured Nancy's status as a series-book superstar.

By 1934 sales of the Nancy Drew novels had skyrocketed. That April, Fortune magazine zeroed in on the unprecedented success of both Nancy and her creator in the widely quoted (and controversial) article "For It Was Indeed He":

> Nancy is the greatest phenomenon among all the fifty-centers (juve-
> nile books). She is a best seller. How she crashed a Valhalla that had been
> rigidly restricted to the male of her species is a mystery even to her pub-
> lishers. . . . Grosset & Dunlap would be well justified in placing atop its
> whimsical 700-mile-high spire a monumental bronze of Mr. (Edward)
> Stratemeyer—for he alone produced 250 miles of it. He was the father of
> this fifty-cent literature.

Nancy was not the first heroine generated by Stratemeyer's
syndicate to join the ranks of the fifty-cent novel, but she was
the first to outsell all of the boys' series characters. She was also
the first to appeal to girls who would have new freedom, including the right to vote, the option of having a career, and the
ability to pursue their dreams without benefit (or limitation) of
an ever-present male protector. Stratemeyer's Nancy did not
cringe at the thought of entering haunted mansions or pursuing sinister villains. She reveled in the excitement of the chase,
and she did so as a full-time detective. Unlike her predecessor
Ruth Fielding, who stumbled upon mysteries en route to her
theatrical career, or later heroines like Cherry Ames, a student
nurse who solved mysteries in between shifts at the hospital,
Nancy performed as River Heights' star sleuth around the
clock.

The Rise and Fall of a Literary Empire

The most ironic part of the Nancy Drew saga is that Edward
Stratemeyer never lived to witness his greatest success. He died
of pneumonia the same spring that the three test ("breeder")
volumes of the series were released.

Stratemeyer left his family a million-dollar empire acknowledged as the major single producer of juvenile books in the
world. His daughters, Harriet and Edna, were called upon to
take over the syndicate, and this responsibility no doubt gave
the sisters pause.

Historians have estimated that Edward Stratemeyer was responsible for twenty-five different series at the time of his
death. He had personally written about two hundred volumes
and edited another eight hundred. Several of his creations, in-

The Stratemeyer family memorial behind his marker is a massive structure formed in the shape of a bookcase, situated amid the memorials of other literary notables, including Stephen Crane, author of *The Red Badge of Courage*, and Mary Mapes Dodge, who created the character Hans Brinker and the story of his silver skates. Ironically, this cemetery is also the burial site of hundreds of nameless orphan children who died penniless in the late nineteenth century—the very prototypes for countless Stratemeyer characters. However, in Edward Stratemeyer's equitable, fictitious world, these children triumphed over the odds and ascended to their rightful glory.

The Stratemeyer family monument is in Evergreen Cemetery, Elizabeth, New Jersey. (Kathleen W. Perletti/*The Star Ledger*)

The Carolyn Keene Trials: Will the Real Ghost of Nancy Drew Please Stand Up?

Until recently, one of the best-kept secrets in literary history was the identity of the original Carolyn Keene. It took half a century, a major court case, and tireless investigating by avid book collectors to discover the truth about Nancy Drew's author. Edward Stratemeyer conceived the idea, but did not actually write the early volumes, so two questions remain: Who wrote the earliest Nancy Drew mysteries, and why are so many people curious about the answer?

Let's begin with the second question.

It is as natural for fans to be intrigued by Nancy Drew's origins as it is for them to crave the "true story" behind the life of any celebrity. Although Nancy is a fictional character, she has accumulated volumes of media coverage since her debut. Articles about Nancy Drew have appeared in virtually every major magazine and newspaper in the United States; she has been a victim of numerous censorship campaigns against children's series books; references to her books pop up frequently in best-selling novels and feature films. Scholars have analyzed Nancy's influence on American women and the controversial personality changes she has undergone since her debut. Curiosity about America's teen sleuth and her author has been building for sixty years.

Was Carolyn Keene anything like Nancy? Where did she get those ideas for the ivory charm and the whispering statue? Was the author's hometown similar to River Heights? Were boyish George Fayne and perky Bess Marvin based on real people? Did

Carolyn Keene ever dream that the character of Nancy Drew would have such a strong impact on readers across the globe?

For the first twenty years of the series, Carolyn Keene was completely shrouded in mystery; from 1950 on she was shrouded in misinformation. Giving in to public pressure, Harriet Stratemeyer Adams, who had taken over her father's literary syndicate after his death in 1930, eventually began to issue press statements addressing the matter of Nancy Drew's author. In hundreds of major publications, in library references such as *Who's Who in Children's Books* and *Something About the Author*, in television broadcasts and at private parties, she let it be known: It was Harriet herself who was Carolyn Keene.

In a typical interview, such as one with *People* magazine in 1977 (shortly after the television debut of the Nancy Drew Mysteries on ABC), Mrs. Adams would state that syndicate series like Tom Swift, Jr., and The Dana Girls were ghostwritten by various free-lance writers, but that *she* was writing the Nancy Drew adventures herself—and had done so since 1930. Occasionally, she would admit that several other people were involved with the editing process, but Harriet Adams proclaimed she wrote every Nancy Drew that rolled off the presses from 1930 to 1982.

In time, this axiom became media gospel. *Newsweek* referred to Adams in 1984, two years after her death, as "the real-life Carolyn Keene for more than half a century." In 1992, *Ms.* magazine called the Hardy Boys and the Nancy Drew novels Harriet Adams's "personal projects, written entirely by her as they had been by her father." But the ghost of the *original* Carolyn Keene was not yet unmasked!

Like her father, Harriet Adams did have an enormous influence on the series; in later years she wrote some of the most coveted volumes. Mrs. Adams was also an outstanding businesswoman who was indisputably linked, psychologically and technically, with Nancy Drew's success for half a century. But Harriet was not the writer who took Edward Stratemeyer's plot outlines and brought Nancy to life. Instead, it was a brilliant young woman from the Midwest, a talented writer who embodied a tremendous portion of Nancy Drew's spirit, daring, and charisma.

She was Mildred Augustine Wirt, now known as Mildred A. Wirt Benson.

The Oath of Secrecy

Mildred Wirt Benson wrote twenty-two of the first twenty-five volumes of the series—those that established Nancy as a superstar. In her own style, Mrs. Benson created distinctive dialogue, named the streets of River Heights, and clothed evildoers like Nathan Gombet in appropriately seedy attire. She steadfastly took a paper-doll sketch of Nancy and produced fifty-thousand-word manuscripts about a full-fledged teen detective which Grosset & Dunlap published with enthusiasm. Authors who later continued or revised the series, including Harriet Adams, did not break ground with a new Nancy Drew. They used the foundation Mildred Wirt Benson had built from 1930 to 1953 to keep Nancy alive for the next generation of readers.

Why was the issue of authorship such a closely guarded secret? What really happened behind the scenes while Nancy was happily sleuthing? And how did such inaccurate information about Nancy Drew, and other syndicate series, remain uncontested for so long? Some of the answers lie in the intricate operations of the Stratemeyer empire as it was ruled by Harriet S. Adams.

As far back as 1905, ghostwriters of syndicate titles routinely received, along with their paychecks, a stiff agreement assigning to the syndicate all claims to authorship, plots, and copyrights to house names. This contract, which some of the writers called "a quasi-blood oath," was not taken lightly, especially during the reign of Harriet Adams. During the Depression and the lean war years following it, syndicate writers were much more concerned about receiving a steady paycheck than about gaining personal recognition, and few dared risk the legal and financial consequences of breaking the syndicate-imposed silence. Even to this day, some writers are reluctant to claim authorship for specific books.

In the embryonic stages of the syndicate, there were two primary reasons for guarding writers' identities. First, the Stratemeyer family believed adamantly that if the public were to find out that Carolyn Keene, Victor Appleton, Franklin W. Dixon, and other authors did not really exist, readers would become disillusioned and it would adversely affect sales. The syndicate believed that readers needed to feel they were purchasing the work of a real person with whom they could identify.

Fifty years after the Nancy Drew series began, this theory altered somewhat. Harriet told numerous interviewers that she felt young girls would be disillusioned if they knew Carolyn Keene (Adams) was an old woman.

The second reason for not disclosing writers' real names was that so many people within the syndicate participated in the development of each book. The Stratemeyers often used an assembly line approach in which the conception, outline, drafting, and editing of each book was done by a different person. This made the question of authorship understandably clouded.

But a third point to consider is that the Stratemeyer family seemed to have a passion for secrecy. Both Edward Stratemeyer and Harriet Adams mastered the art of maintaining a public image while holding back the details of how they grossed their millions, or the reasoning behind their business decisions—which was, of course, their option.

Even steady employees weren't aware of everything that was transpiring. Jim Lawrence, who conceived the Chris Cool series and wrote or revised at least 125 syndicate titles, including numerous Tom Swift, Jr. books, began working closely with Harriet in the 1950s—yet he had not heard of Mildred Wirt Benson or known of her involvement with the Nancy Drew books until 1980. "I'm not sure, really, why Mrs. Benson wasn't mentioned as author of those early volumes," Mr. Lawrence said. "One just didn't talk about such things with Mrs. Adams. Certain topics, especially those dealing with Nancy Drew, were taboo." The enormous respect that he and other employees felt for Harriet Adams persuaded them to accept her preference for a "closed-door mentality" concerning syndicate business dealings.

Syndicate administrators would deal with most writers exclusively through the mail and would stagger personal appointments in the company's office so that writers couldn't meet and exchange war stories. Harriet and her primary partner, Andrew Svenson, established a firm line between free-lance writers and full-time staff writers. A strict period of apprenticeship was required, sometimes over a period of years, before a writer could make the transition from free-lance to full-time. This way, only the most trusted were allowed into the syndicate's hallowed halls.

The Case of the Missing Records

One of the most intriguing mysteries can be found, or shall we say not found, in the U.S. Copyright Office. In an article for *Yellowback Library* entitled "Carolyn Keene, pseud." (1984), Geoffrey S. Lapin pointed out that the government records concerning Nancy Drew are particularly puzzling: "Someone has unofficially been purging the Copyright Office records of all information ever kept by them concerning those who had done work in some capacity for the old Stratemeyer Syndicate."

During Lapin's laborious twenty-year search for the identity of Carolyn Keene, he learned that in the mid-1930s, syndicate author Walter Karig broke precedent and his contract by sending to the Library of Congress a list of all the books he had ghostwritten for the syndicate. He listed two Nancy Drew titles (he did indeed write two or three), but later "an overzealous cataloger" assumed that all Drew books, volumes 1 through 14, had been written by Walter Karig. This caused quite a flurry, both at the syndicate and at the publishers, Grosset & Dunlap, and it took years to straighten out this mistake.

When Lapin was doing research in 1982 at the U.S. Copyright Office, he found and photocopied a 1937 reference card that read: "Keene, Carolyn, pseud., see Karig, Walter, 1898–; Real name not to be disclosed under any circumstances." There was a special addendum to the card that read: "(Letter in Mr. Leavitt's office.)" Another card, apparently inserted into the files after the Karig misunderstanding was resolved, stated "Keene, Carolyn, pseud.," with a line through "Karig, Walter, 1898–."

Strangely enough, when Lapin returned to the Library of Congress in the late 1980s, those cards were missing from the files! And when he inquired about a former employee named Mr. Leavitt, he was told there was no record of the man's employment.

However, one of Lapin's most disheartening discoveries was that almost all first-edition Nancy Drew Mystery Stories were missing from the archives of the Library of Congress. (Thanks to his diligent efforts and personal donations, the library's series-book collection archives have been replenished.)

Regardless of the absence of public records, the names of ghostwriters and the secrets of the syndicate itself eventually began to leak out. In the 1966 book *My Father Was Uncle Wiggly* (McGraw-Hill) Roger Garis outlined the ghostwriting activities of his entire family. He, his sister Cleo, and both their parents,

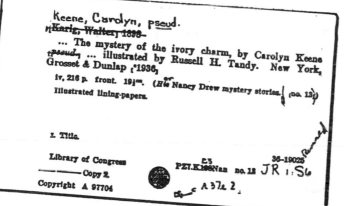

These Library of Congress cards document one writer's interest in going on record as an author of the Nancy Drew Mystery Stories.

Howard and Lillian, had done an enormous amount of work for the syndicate, and *Uncle Wiggly* allowed readers a rare glimpse behind the scenes. Leslie McFarlane wrote an informative and entertaining autobiography called *The Ghost of the Hardy Boys* for Methuen Publishing in 1976, telling of his work for the syndicate and admitting he was the original Franklin W. Dixon of Hardy Boys fame.

But Mildred Wirt Benson, the ghost of Nancy Drew, remained true to the contract she had signed in the late 1920s. She never publicly disclosed that she was the first Carolyn Keene and never used the name for personal gain. Mrs. Benson admits today that she rarely even thought about the matter—until she received a subpoena to testify from the U.S. District Court of New York.

In 1979, after a seventy-five-year relationship between Grosset & Dunlap and the syndicate, Harriet Adams apparently decided that the syndicate was not getting a fair share of the series' royalties and that she wanted a more innovative approach to marketing the "big three": Nancy Drew, The Hardy Boys, and The Bobbsey Twins. According to *Publishers Weekly* (May 14, 1979), Adams had recently announced that she was considering the publication of new titles in these series with another publisher—Simon & Schuster. In response, Grosset & Dunlap filed a multimillion-dollar, multiple-complaint lawsuit against both the Stratemeyer Syndicate and Simon & Schuster. In part, Grosset & Dunlap felt they had exclusive rights to publish these series (as well as joint copyright ownership) because they had provided the books' illustrations since 1904. Grosset & Dunlap also charged that Simon & Schuster had intentionally and wrongfully interfered with their prior contract negotiations with the Stratemeyer Syndicate.

Therefore, in 1980, her fiftieth-anniversary year, Nancy Drew was plunged into one of the major publishing battles of all time—one that would change the series, and the syndicate, forever.

The trial, which ran from May 27 to June 12, 1980, dealt with many issues, the most prominent of which was who *did* have the right to publish the Nancy Drew mysteries. Through the extensive personal testimonies of both Harriet S. Adams and Mildred Wirt Benson, the case also clarified the identities of the original and subsequent Carolyn Keenes.

In the end, Nancy was both divided and conquered. This is why fans are often confused when they see Nancy Drew mysteries surface in both hard and soft cover, with blatantly different styles of illustration and text. In 1980 Grosset & Dunlap was awarded exclusive hardcover print rights (in English) to the original Nancy Drew volumes #1 through #56. Simon & Schuster took over Nancy's new titles in paperback (and introduced her updated look) from volume #57 on, and eventually launched the Nancy Drew Files, River Heights USA, and other spin-off series. When Simon & Schuster and its parent company bought the syndicate in 1984, it took over the trademark to the Nancy Drew Mystery Stories and retained Grosset & Dunlap as the licensed publisher of Nancy Drew hardcover volumes 1 through 56.

Today, the copyright and licensing policies of the Nancy Drew series are still undergoing changes, but the behind-the-scenes operations remain much the same: the Nancy Drew Mystery Stories and their spin-off series are penned by numerous ghostwriters under the name Carolyn Keene. The process is handled by Mega-Books, a major New York packaging house that also handles other Simon & Schuster series, including The Hardy Boys, The Bobbsey Twins, and Tom Swift, Jr.

But technicalities aside, the single most important outcome of that trial, for Nancy Drew fans, was that Mildred Wirt Benson was finally recognized as the original Carolyn Keene.

In a letter to the editor in Publishers Weekly (September 26, 1986), Mrs. Benson responded to an article she believed had misrepresented the Nancy Drew series. It read, in part: "Years ago, when I tapped out the opening lines of the first Nancy Drew mystery ever written, I never dreamed that I would spend most of my life defending it. . . . Does authorship really matter? Probably not, but loyal Nancy Drew fans, especially the earliest readers, deserve true information, rather than slanted or incorrect publicity statements."

And what of the other mystery? Why did Harriet S. Adams deny Mildred Wirt Benson her due, even after it became public knowledge that Carolyn Keene was a pseudonym? No one is quite certain. The topic wasn't discussed, even at the trial in 1980. In one of her interviews with researcher Geoffrey S.

Lapin, Mildred Wirt Benson mentioned that when she and Harriet Adams finally met, in the New York courts, Harriet's only comment to Mrs. Benson was, "I thought you were dead."

The history of Nancy Drew is clouded with questions that will probably never be answered. Further complications in the quest for truth are surfacing daily as more information is made public. For example, book collector and author John Dizer said in a telephone interview that he experienced no problems at all with secrecy while researching Edward Stratemeyer's work and life and investigating the names of individuals behind syndicate pseudonyms. Dizer said he was greeted graciously, even encouraged by Harriet Adams and her assistant Nancy Axelrad to help them piece together the complex story of the syndicate. According to Dizer, the idea of a full-blown cover-up regarding syndicate house names has been over-dramatized.

Still, substantial evidence exists to prove that when it came to Nancy Drew, the authorship question was always of deep concern with the Stratemeyer Syndicate. If it hadn't been, the Superior Court trial of 1980 over the rights to publish Nancy Drew would not have dealt so extensively with the question of who really wrote which Nancy Drew titles.

Perhaps the biggest challenge to presenting a balanced, truthful history is the tendency of fans and collectors to disagree on such questions as: Which author wrote more Nancys? Who was the first? Who was the best? Who was the real Carolyn Keene?

In any case, it is easy to see that Edward Stratemeyer, Harriet S. Adams, and Mildred Wirt Benson were each one of a triad responsible for helping Nancy Drew attain (and retain) her best-seller status.

Edward Stratemeyer conceived Nancy Drew, acting as her official literary sire and providing her with a powerful financial base as she greeted the world. Mildred Wirt Benson breathed life into her, forming Nancy's spirit, personality, and feminist pluck. Harriet Adams played the role of dedicated foster parent, guiding Nancy through the trials of her series' adolescence, in-

The Carolyn Keene Trials: Will the Real Ghost of Nancy Drew Please Stand Up?

31

troducing her to international intrigue, and helping her adjust to society's changing perspective.

And Nancy's current publisher is the capable inheritor, making certain Nancy proceeds into the next century with equal doses of spirit and savvy while retaining her loyal readership.

The Carolyn Keenes Unmasked

Mildred Augustine Wirt Benson

I used to hang my hammock in Mayan Temples, and once, when no shelter was available, I hung it in a corn crib. . . . On a trip from Palenque, Mexico, to a jungle near the Guatemalan frontier, I landed on a river bank and went down it in a dug-out canoe with native paddlemen.

Mildred Wirt Benson, the original "Carolyn Keene," pages through her first Nancy Drew mystery at her Ohio home. Behind her is the typewriter she used while writing the manuscript. (Geoffrey S. Lapin)

The previous passage, from Geoffrey S. Lapin's article "Carolyn Keene, pseud.," is not a fictional excerpt from a Nancy Drew mystery, but a bona fide experience from the life of "Carolyn Keene." For fans who wonder if the original Nancy Drew author was as spirited and daring as Nancy Drew herself, the answer is an indisputable yes.

Mildred Augustine, born July 10, 1905, in Ladora, Iowa, developed an early interest in archaeology that eventually led her away from her peaceful hometown and into exotic international locales. When Mildred tired of hiring bush pilots to transport her to remote digs, she piloted herself in her own Piper Cherokee (she has six different licenses, including one for seaplaning). Mildred took to the skies in an era when most other young women were preparing for a career in homemaking. So zealous was she about aeronautics that she eventually modeled an entire series of juvenile novels, the Ruth Darrow Flying Stories, on the life of aviator Ruth Elder.

Mildred Augustine was an academic pioneer as well: she was the first woman to graduate from the School of Journalism at the University of Iowa, and in 1927 she also earned that university's first master's degree in journalism. She confesses, however, that she was writing books when she was supposed to be writing her thesis.

Today, at age eighty-eight, she still likes to fly and play golf, writes a weekly column called "On the Go" for the Toledo *Blade,* and takes pride in the fulfillment of her girlhood dream of becoming a published author. Her first short story sold when she was only thirteen, and since then she has written more than 130 children's books. Her pseudonyms include Julia K. Duncan, Don Palmer, Frances K. Judd, and Helen Louise Thorndyke (of the Honey Bunch series), but it was under her own name, Mildred A. Wirt, that she created her personal favorite, the Penny Parker series. Ironically, writing the Nancy Drew mysteries was a small part of Mildred's life, undertaken simply to help pay the bills.

It all started around 1926, when she boarded a train headed for the center of the American publishing industry, New York City. There she met Edward Stratemeyer, who had advertised for ghostwriters for his literary syndicate. Mildred showed him stories she had written that had appeared in St. *Nicholas Magazine* and *Lutheran Young Folks,* then returned home with Stratemeyer's promise that she might be contacted "sometime in the future." Her first book for the syndicate was *Ruth Fielding and Her Great Scenario*, written under the name Alice B. Emerson. She wrote a number of additional books in that series until 1929, when Stratemeyer mailed her a brief outline about a new teen sleuth named Nancy Drew. Within two months, Mildred completed *The Secret of the Old Clock* and mailed her manuscript to the syndicate.

But alas, her employer was not pleased.

In *Library Lit. 20—The Best of 1989*, Mildred Wirt said, "Mr. Stratemeyer expressed bitter disappointment when he received the manuscript, saying the heroine was much too flip, and would never be well received." But publishers Grosset & Dunlap disagreed and requested two more Drew titles to be released in the spring of 1930 as "breeder" (test) volumes. Nancy was an overnight success, and Mildred soon received an outline for the fourth volume, *The Mystery at Lilac Inn* (1930), the last book she wrote for the syndicate before Edward died. Later that same year, Harriet S. Adams took over the plot outlines for new Drew titles.

Over time, these outlines progressed from a few paragraphs to numerous pages—often blocking Mildred's creative flow. Still, she kept writing until the syndicate informed her, at the height of the Great Depression, that she would have to take a pay cut to seventy-five dollars per book, fifty dollars less than her usual rate. She refused, and volumes #8, #9, and #10 were written by Walter Karig. Mildred returned for volume #11, *The Clue of the Broken Locket* (1934), and continued through volume #25, *The Ghost of Blackwood Hall* (1948). Her final Drew title was *The Clue of the Velvet Mask* in 1953. After that, her work with the syndicate and their acknowledgment of her existence ceased.

Was Nancy Drew based on a specific person Mildred Wirt Benson knew? Was Nancy Drew autobiographical? The answer to both of these questions is no. Yet much of the writer's life experience and her spunky, versatile character found its way into the plots. When Mildred wrote *The Bungalow Mystery* (1930), for example, she was working as a swimming instructor, and in the book we find Nancy teaching her friend Helen Corning how to swim. Mildred's fondness for aviation was incorporated into *The Clue in the Crumbling Wall* (1945), in which Nancy becomes an experienced pilot. And although fans have speculated for years about the location of River Heights, Betsy Caprio's book *The Mystery of Nancy Drew* (1992) notes that Mrs. Benson definitely had Iowa in mind for Nancy's hometown. Mildred was a true heroine of the Midwest, just like Nancy, and her early descriptions of the scenic cornfields and vast rivers of fictional River Heights illustrate her pride and appreciation of the land.

The strongest influence of Mildred Wirt Benson surfaced in Nancy's spirit, personality, and independence. The author admits she was rather industrious for her time, even a twenties "flapper" of sorts, and never let her gender stop her from striving to reach her goals. In a biographical article for *Books at Iowa* (1989), Mildred wrote that since she had to comply with the often "hackneyed names and situations" forwarded to her by the syndicate, she instead "concentrated hard on *Nancy*, trying to make her a departure from the stereotyped heroine of my day." She felt those girls were too silly and made an active effort to depict Nancy as intelligent, agile, and resourceful. Anita Sue Grossman reported in *Ohio* magazine (1987) that Mildred attributed the appeal of Nancy Drew to a wish-fulfillment fantasy. Mildred purposely supplied Nancy with certain qualities that she felt had been lacking in her own late teens, such as "exceptional good looks, an oversupply of college dates and great freedom to do as she pleased." If Mildred hoped to combine these "wish I were" qualities with the very real independent leanings of her own character, she certainly succeeded.

Also, like Nancy, Mildred is gifted with staunch determination. She could withstand enormous career pressure and was never the type to give in to life's challenges. In 1936, Mildred (then Mildred A. Wirt), produced ten books and also gave birth to a baby girl. By the mid-1940s she was writing up to twelve titles a year, working as a journalist, dealing with motherhood, and nursing her husband, who had suffered a stroke. "I set up my typewriter beside his bed," Mildred recalled in *Ohio*, "and I was writing these different stories . . . half-through the night. If they sound tired, they were tired." But, as Grossman pointed out, one of Mildred's best titles, *Swamp Island*, appeared in 1947, the same year her first husband, Asa Wirt, died. Even during times of great stress Mildred persevered.

Her enormous literary output continued through the late 1940s. In 1950 she married George A. Benson, then editor for the *Toledo Blade*. George died in 1959, but Mildred continued working at that paper, as she does to this day. Through the years, she has received numerous awards for her accomplishments as a journalist, including the 1989 Ohio Newspaper Women's Citation for feature writing.

Mildred's last book was *Quarry Ghost*, published by Dodd, Mead and Company in 1959. By then, Mildred no doubt saw the numerous media stories depicting Harriet S. Adams as the only Carolyn Keene, but she did not break the oath of silence she had sealed with Edward Stratemeyer until the 1980 trial, *Grosset & Dunlap* vs. *Simon & Schuster and the Stratemeyer Syndicate*.

Since then, series-book historians including Geoffrey S. Lapin, Ernie Kelly, David Farah, and others have worked hard to assemble the facts of Mildred's career (as well as the facts about other Stratemeyer Syndicate ghostwriters) in order to bring the true Carolyn Keene out of the shadows.

In an interview for *Yellowback Library* in 1983, Mildred Wirt Benson told Geoffrey S. Lapin: "Even if I didn't get it across to the Court, I know who wrote those books, and I set up the form which made Nancy Drew top sellers. . . . Fact is, my old typewriter, which I still have, has keys completely worn down from use. I'm not proud of any of the writing, but I think I did come through with a different concept, now accepted as common."

Sixty-two years after she wrote the first Nancy Drew mystery story, Mildred Wirt Benson received the Lifetime Achievement Award from the Society of Phantom Friends, an organization of adult collectors of girls' series books. The University of Iowa, her alma mater, also houses a large collection of juvenile series books, including those written by Benson.

In 1991 the respected reference book *Something About the Author* (volume 65) listed Mrs. Benson's massive literary accomplishments, and for the first time, it included a cross-reference to "Carolyn Keene."

Harriet Stratemeyer Adams

When Edward Stratemeyer died in 1930 he left his family an enormous literary empire and an equally enormous dilemma. His wife, Magdalene, herself advanced in years, hadn't an inkling of how her husband had managed to orchestrate the hundreds of series titles he was currently producing for major publishers. That left Edward's daughters, Harriet and Edna, to

**Harriet Stratemeyer Adams,
circa 1930.**

inherit his business. Edna's formal involvement with the syndicate ended almost as swiftly as it began, but Harriet was truly her father's daughter.

The way Harriet S. Adams handled employees was sometimes called unethical by competing publishers and by several syndicate ghostwriters who felt they were never given ample credit (or ample financial compensation) for their work. But Harriet was also known as a remarkably tenacious, capable businesswoman who kept her father's empire running until her death in 1982. And there is no controversy whatsoever concerning the heartfelt devotion and meticulous effort she gave to the Nancy Drew series.

Harriet took full control of the syndicate when she was in her late thirties, backed by a degree from Wellesley College (class of 1914) but lacking any substantial business experience. As the wife of an investment banker and the mother of four young children, she was busy at that point with family and social obligations, not contract negotiations and boilerplates. In numerous interviews, Harriet stated she had assisted her father from time to time in his office—but never administratively. And she had never published a book. Against all odds of succeeding, Harriet accepted the gauntlet, and by her fortieth birthday, her entire life had changed.

Harriet's first step was to move the syndicate's offices from Manhattan to East Orange, New Jersey (a much closer commute to her northeastern New Jersey home). She fired and hired various employees, organized her own production schedule, and decided to concentrate on the syndicate's biggest money-makers: The Hardy Boys, The Bobbsey Twins, and Nancy Drew. When Harriet took over the company, Grosset & Dunlap requested that Mildred Wirt Benson continue writing the Nancy Drew mysteries. Harriet complied, but the outlines she sent to Mildred for that series became longer, the grammatical reins tighter. After Mildred's last title for the Nancy Drew series was written, in 1953, Harriet officially became the new Carolyn Keene.

Like her predecessor, the new Carolyn Keene had spirit and an independent nature, but Harriet also had an intense emotional attachment to Nancy Drew. In numerous interviews, Mildred admitted that she viewed her writing of Nancy Drew books as a job, while Harriet regarded Nancy as a daughter. In an article in *Publishers Weekly* (May 30, 1986) by Diane Roback, Grosset & Dunlap editor Doris Duenewald (who oversaw the Nancy Drew books in the early 1960s) said of Harriet Adams: "Harriet had her own little world—and it was a lovely one. She felt very close to Nancy." That same article pointed out that Adams often referred to Nancy "as a daughter." This is supported by Jim Lawrence, a former syndicate staff writer, who said (in a phone interview with the author): "I greatly respected Harriet Adams, although she got a bit odd in her old age—sometimes fancying herself Nancy Drew—at least the mother of Nancy Drew. The series was always her baby, so to speak, and her outlines and research for that series were always meticulous."

Harriet's possessiveness, and the stringent rules relating to the Nancy Drew Mystery Stories, are legendary. Harriet's personality was more reserved than Mildred Wirt Benson's, making Harriet's depiction of Nancy Drew more restrained as well. Nancy's brassy qualities were toned down, the texts became noticeably shorter and, some readers feel, rather homogenized— Nancy became a scaled-down version of a supersleuth. In the late 1950s Harriet engineered a mammoth undertaking—the revision of all the original Nancy Drew texts, a process that lasted twenty-five years. The extent of these revisions varied from book to book; sometimes one sentence was deleted, other times an entirely new plot was devised. Harriet changed Nancy's blue roadster to a blue convertible, updated iceboxes to refrigerators, and most important, eliminated the abundant ethnic stereotypes that marred the original volumes.

Harriet loved to travel, and she wove many of her experiences into the new and revised titles. According to Stratemeyer Syndicate chronologer Ernie Kelly ("Inside the Stratemeyer Syndicate," 1988, *Yellowback Library*), Harriet traveled to the Far East in 1959; soon after, Nancy traveled to Hong Kong in *The Mystery of the Fire Dragon* (1961). Harriet also visited Istanbul, South America, and Scotland, all sites where Nancy and company later became entangled in intrigue. Many fans fondly recall Nancy's visit to Scotland to find her genealogical roots in *The Clue of the Whistling Bagpipes* (1964) and her trek to exotic Istanbul in *The Mysterious Mannequin* (1970). Harriet also enjoyed imparting educational information to her readers, and the titles she wrote as Carolyn Keene were peppered with interesting facts and legends—everything from the tales of a one-eyed Cyclops and methods of deciphering codes to techniques of Kabuki theater.

A few other syndicate authors made contributions to the Nancy Drew series, but first drafts and editing always were based on Harriet's detailed outlines, under her close supervision. Margaret Scherf Beebe and Iris Vinton contributed to the series in the 1950s (see box).

Beginning in 1965, Harriet worked with one assistant in particular, Nancy Axelrad, who eventually became her business partner. (It's interesting to note that Ms. Axelrad's first name was Nancy, and she graduated from Drew University. No doubt Mrs. Adams considered this a good omen.) For a brief time following Harriet's death, several articles, including one for

Margaret Sherf Beebe (1908–1979) was one of the few writers of the Nancy Drew Mystery Stories during the reign of Harriet S. Adams. Researcher Ernie Kelly learned that Beebe was a major contributor to *The Secret of the Golden Pavilion* (1959) and *The Clue in the Old Stagecoach* (1960). Beebe published numerous detective novels; her juvenile book for Watts, *The Mystery of the Shaky Staircase* (1965), featured a heroine named Harriet Adams! This publicity photo of Margaret Sherf Beebe by Maurice Roy appears courtesy of the Montana Historical Society, Helena.

Iris Vinton (1905–1988) contributed to *The Secret of the Wooden Lady* (1950) and *The Clue of the Black Keys* (1951). Ms. Vinton prepared her own obituary for the *New York Times*, listing publicly, for the first time, her ghostwriting for the Stratemeyer Syndicate. Vinton was an accomplished children's author; one of her books, *Flying Ebony*, was made into a film for Walt Disney under the title *The Mooncussers*. She was noted for her stories about ships and juvenile biographies of famous historical personalities. This line drawing of Iris Vinton by Addison Burbank appears courtesy of Ernie Kelly.

Newsweek in 1984 by David Gates, referred to Axelrod as the "new Carolyn Keene."

For thirty years, Harriet S. Adams was in total control of the Nancy Drew series. Her recognition as Carolyn Keene peaked in 1980, Nancy Drew's fiftieth anniversary, when Harriet was honored internationally for her achievements as a female role model and a contributor to the field of children's fiction. The largest event of the anniversary season was a party hosted by Simon & Schuster in April 1980. The jubilee generated widespread publicity for both Nancy and her author, with such newspapers as the *Washington Post* reporting the details of the gala—complete with quotes from notable Nancy Drew fans including Barbara Walters, Joan Mondale, and Beverly Sills.

Over the course of her career, Harriet S. Adams edited more than five hundred books for the syndicate and wrote one hundred titles herself (including many Bobbsey Twins and Dana Girls books). She was a disciplined, prolific author in her own right who certainly earned her entry in the New Jersey literary hall of fame.

Harriet was fond of saying that her depiction of Nancy Drew was governed by the Wellesley College motto: *Non Ministrari Sed Ministrare* ("Not to be ministered unto, but to minister"). This motto obviously applied not only to Nancy, but to Harriet as well. As the second Carolyn Keene, she found time to write most of the titles even as she presided over both the Nancy Drew series and her father's entire business with an iron fist. Those who worked with her at the syndicate agreed that Nancy Drew was always number one with Harriet Stratemeyer Adams.

Nancy Drew Through the Decades: Her Covers and Cover Artists

It was 1929, and the history of girls' series books was about to change forever.

The manuscripts of *The Secret of the Old Clock*, *The Hidden Staircase*, and *The Bungalow Mystery* were completed and ready. Grosset & Dunlap needed a strong visual enticement to convince Depression-ravaged readers to part with their money. This new series had to stand out among thousands of other fifty-cent juvenile titles vying for America's attention. With the books scheduled for a spring 1930 release, Nancy Drew had to be transformed into living color, *fast*.

Grosset & Dunlap responded by hiring one of the best commercial illustrators in New York City to design the dust jackets for the Nancy Drew Mystery Stories. Russell Haviland Tandy's unique artistic style was the perfect match for the lively writing of Mildred Wirt Benson (pseudonym Carolyn Keene).

Tandy was the first in a long line of illustrators who brought Nancy Drew to life. Like the text, the cover art and the internal line drawings have undergone drastic changes through the decades. Styles have shifted along with social trends, the whims of art directors, and the budgets of the publishers. Most important, the varying results reflect the unique personalities of the artists themselves. Nancy Drew's illustrators left such highly distinctive marks on the series that it can now be divided into equally distinctive artistic eras.

Which Nancy Drew do you remember?

Russell Tandy's inspiration for the original Nancy Drew was a professional New York model named Grace Horton. This rare line sketch of Miss Horton from 1940 shows the striking resemblance between the model and the image of Nancy Drew as she appeared on this cover from 1944. (Sketch, John Tandy/Cover, Simon & Schuster)

1930–1950: Classic Ethereal Nancy

Russell H. Tandy was responsible for twenty-five dust jackets designed from 1930 to 1950. He also drew most of the exquisitely detailed frontispieces and interior illustrations that dreamy-eyed girls stared at for hours, searching for clues to Nancy's appearance.

Tandy gave us a sophisticated girl/woman set against intriguing backdrops that hinted at the story beneath the cover. The intermingling of her halo of golden curls, her vivid blue eyes, and her lithe physique, executed in watercolor wash, resulted in Classic Ethereal Nancy.

Nancy exuded an all-American quality, due in part to the artist's preference for red, white, and blue. Tandy personally read every text before he began sketching, so his early covers were closely connected to specific scenes in the plots. He also hand painted the cover lettering, an art in itself.

Fans from this era fondly recall Nancy's clothes and accessories, and with good reason. Tandy was an accomplished fashion illustrator and always dressed Nancy Drew in ultra-chic designs. Her hairstyle reflected that period's look, and her shapely, long legs rivaled Betty Grable's.

Nancy of the thirties wore cloches, white gloves, three-quarter-length skirts, and strapped stiletto heels. Her face was heart-shaped, her brows finely lined. In the glossy illustrations of early-numbered volumes, Nancy exudes the poise of a runway model, as sophisticated in a Victorian drawing room as she is sprawled at the bottom of a darkened stairwell.

From 1930 to 1936, Nancy Drew volumes #1 through #13 included a glossy frontispiece and three glossy interior line drawings by Tandy. Unfortunately, beginning in 1937 the three glossy interior drawings were dropped from the books, so few contemporary fans have ever seen them. (In later years some editions included interior drawings, but not the original Tandy versions.) The glossy frontispieces, however, were retained through 1943, after which time they were produced on plain paper, as they are to this day in most reprints of Nancy Drew hardcovers.

Nancy goes to work on her first case in this frontispiece from *The Secret of the Old Clock* (1930). Her sophisticated pose and chic clothes typify Tandy's Classic Ethereal Nancy Drew. (Simon & Schuster)

The Nancy Drew silhouette of the 1930s included a scarf around Nancy's neck and a shadow at her feet. (Simon & Schuster)

In the 1940s Nancy's hair was less curly and sometimes was arranged in a French knot. Her clothing tended to be tailored ensembles popular during the war years, and she wore low-heeled pumps. The background scenes moved steadily toward the gothic, with rich, colorful pictures of mansions, ghostly figures, and dastardly villains lurking in the distance.

Perhaps Tandy's most memorable work was the now-famous silhouette of the famous sleuth peering into her magnifying glass. There were two versions of this design: the second, introduced circa 1947, did away with the scarf around Nancy's neck and the shadow at her feet. To this day, even nonreaders of Nancy Drew mysteries can identify her by this silhouette, which appeared on the cover of the blue hardbacks until 1962.

Tandy's final cover for the Nancy Drew Mystery Stories was *The Clue of the Leaning Chimney* (1949), which featured Nancy, Bess Marvin, and George Fayne peering across a fence toward a ram-

Russell Haviland Tandy:
The First Nancy Drew Cover Artist

Russell Haviland Tandy was born in Brooklyn, New York, in 1893. His artistic talents surfaced early on and he attended the Art Students' League in New York City. After he graduated, he became a free-lance commercial artist. In 1917 he began to illustrate the cover packages for Butterick sewing patterns, then progressed to illustrating catalog ads for Sears, Montgomery Ward, and J. C. Penney. During the 1920s he published his only book, *Tandy's Babies*, which earned him an esteemed reputation for children's portraiture.

Tandy was a good friend of Edward Stratemeyer, who helped the artist enter the book illustration field in 1929. Tandy worked for publishers Grosset & Dunlap and Cupples & Leon. For twenty years Tandy illustrated many covers for the Nancy Drew, Hardy Boys, Buddy Books, and Dana Girls series, as well as other series.

Tandy was quite talented in oil painting as well. In 1940 he won first prize in a New York City art competition in which each artist, working with oil paints, had four hours to produce a piece of art. Tandy's painting, *The Ruffian*, beat the entries of Norman Rockwell, McClelland Barclay, and Tandy's longtime drinking companion, Salvador Dali.

When Tandy was fifteen, a serious case of pneumonia left him almost completely deaf. In spite of this he eventually became an accomplished band director

Russell Haviland Tandy
(Courtesy of Geoffrey S. Lapin)

and trumpet soloist, performing with the Edwin Franco Goldman Band. He also did ghostwriting for Franco and created two of the band's hit songs, "On the Mall" and "En Garde."

Noted for his feisty and artistic temperament, Tandy reputedly would turn off his hearing aid whenever he wanted to ignore what was being said to him, but he was known for his generosity as well, especially during the Depression. He gave to the less fortunate whenever possible, and often entertained young neighbors with sketches and games. His granddaughter Pam recalled that as a child she would have him autograph Nancy Drew books as birthday presents for her friends, saying, "My grandfather drew the pictures!"

From 1950 to 1960 Tandy worked as a commercial artist for major New York department stores, including Lord & Taylor and Saks Fifth Avenue. He then retired with his second wife, Irene, to his custom-designed home in Sarasota, Florida, which was decorated with much of his original artwork and a prized sofa once owned by Al Capone.

Unfortunately, Tandy died after spending only one year in his dream house.

Today, original dust jackets by Russell Haviland Tandy for the Nancy Drew Mystery Stories are prized by collectors.

Adapted with permission of Geoffrey S. Lapin from his article "Carolyn Keene, pseud.," *Yellowback Library*, March/April 1984.

bling house with a strange chimney. Tandy covers and frontispieces were still used in some printings of the series until the mid-1960s.

In 1962 a fire struck the Tandy home in Sarasota, Florida, just one year after the artist's death. The blaze destroyed virtually all the original paintings and countless illustrations from Tandy's fifty-year career. The only artworks remaining were those he had given to friends and family and a few pieces that had been retained by the Stratemeyer Syndicate. Of the Nancy Drew line, only two sketches of model Grace Horton and the oil paintings from *The Mystery of the Moss-Covered Mansion* (1941) and *The Secret in the Old Attic* (1944) are known to have survived.

The absence of the original paintings make the early dust jackets, particularly those signed by Tandy, extremely valuable to collectors. Texts with dust jackets from the early 1930s print runs command up to five hundred dollars each.

The beautiful work of Russell Haviland Tandy lives on in readers' memories, and collectors' bookshelves, as a wonderful slice of Americana—all produced for a mere seventy-five dollars per painting!

1950–1965: Bobby-Soxer Nancy

The next artists to join the Nancy Drew bandwagon were Bill Gillies, Polly Bolian, and Rudy Nappi. Bill Gillies is said to have revised at least seven of the original Tandy dust jackets in the early 1950s, including *The Secret of the Wooden Lady* (1950) and *The Clue of the Black Keys* (1951). He also designed the "blue digger endpapers," showing Nancy standing on the left, looking from behind a tree at a man digging.

Artist Polly Bolian is responsible for the Nancy Drew Cameo Editions, a limited-edition series featuring stunning watercolor depictions from thirteen Nancy Drew titles, a full-color frontispiece, and nine black-and-white interior drawings. Dust-jacketed "Cameos" are now highly prized by collectors for the outstanding artwork.

It was Rudy Nappi, however, who had the most impact on the series from 1950 to 1979. Like Russell H. Tandy's, Rudy Nappi's formal training stemmed from the Art Students' League in New York City, and he had designed countless covers for mass-market monthlies like *Detective Magazine*. In 1953 Nappi began working for Grosset & Dunlap. He designed more Stratemeyer Syndicate picture book covers, including those for the Hardy Boys, Happy Hollisters, and Nancy Drew series, than any other artist: 150 covers over a thirty-year period. Nappi was with the Drews for so long he eventually had to update his own covers!

With the change in artists and the changes in times came changes in Nancy. Beginning with volume #30, *The Clue of the Velvet Mask* (1953), Nancy Drew's resemblance to movie stars like Carole Lombard was replaced with a new look: Nancy the bobby-soxer. As the years progressed, Nancy took on physical characteristics of Barbie, Gidget, and Doris Day. Unlike Tandy's mature, sophisticated miss, Bobby-Soxer Nancy looked much more like a contemporary sixteen-year-old. Nappi made her perkier, clean-cut, and extremely animated. In the majority of his covers Nancy looks startled—which, no doubt, she was.

Artist Rudy Nappi holds a Nancy Drew book with a cover he designed. (Ernie Kelly)

Nappi also mastered the art of slipping villains and ghosts into the background scenes of the covers, a device he used frequently throughout his association with the syndicate.

In a 1991 interview for *Yellowback Library*, Rudy Nappi said that when he first began the job at Grosset & Dunlap, the art director had specifically asked him to update Nancy's appearance, especially her clothes. Nappi did so, dressing Nancy in 1950s Peter Pan collars, shirtwaist dresses, and simple blouse-and-skirt ensembles. She occasionally wore jeans, and once, in *The Hidden Window Mystery* (1956), she was dressed in a red bathrobe and red polka-dotted flannel pajamas, shining a flashlight on a giant peacock. Rudy Nappi's Bobby-Soxer Nancy was a natural reflection of the 1950s and early '60s fascination for carefree, wide-eyed girls, oozing innocence.

1965–1979: *Trendy Nancy*

During the later 1960s and the '70s, America was undergoing major political and sociological changes. Technology was moving toward the computer age and the women's liberation movement was in full swing. Once again, it was time to alter Nancy Drew. Rudy Nappi, still the primary cover artist, gave us Trendy Nancy. Yet Nancy ventured only so far into the tumultuous rebellion surrounding her.

When the "flip" haircut was all the rage in the 1960s, Nancy's hair was redone to fit right in. But when the baby-boom generation started to wear peace-sign jewelry and plastic love beads, Nancy stayed with simple pearls and gold bracelets. Occasionally the internal line drawings, most of them done by uncredited artists, allowed us a glimpse of the Woodstock-era ambience by showing Nancy and friends dressed in blue jeans or bell-bottom pants.

The primary change in the Nancy Drew artwork during the counterculture era was the replacement of detailed, portrait-style covers with simpler scenes. The hallmark for Trendy Nancy covers was the use of vivid color and the inclusion of nonhuman entities. In *The Crooked Banister* (1971), for example, Nappi chose a glaring psychedelic pink background for a scene of Nancy being accosted by a robot. In *Mystery of the Glowing Eye*

(1974), a large Cyclops eye loomed over Nancy's titian-toned head.

Grosset & Dunlap always chose the scene to be illustrated on the cover and provided Nappi with brief specifications. He didn't read the books, but did pass them along to his wife, who gave him a summary of the plot. From that information, Nappi did a rough pencil sketch, then shot photos of the pose, before he started to paint on canvas. Like many artists, he used props to obtain the right effect.

Nappi was with the Stratemeyer Syndicate during the change from dust jackets to the picture-cover format for the series. The yellow-spine hardcovers hit the stands in 1962, and Nappi revised many of the original covers from the 1930s and '40s during this period. His last Drew cover was *The Thirteenth Pearl* in 1979. Today, he works as a free-lance commercial artist in Pennsylvania.

What's this—Nancy Drew smoking? No, it's a studio shot for the cover of *The Clue of the Whistling Bagpipes* (1964). The model used a cigarette to purse her lips as if she were blowing into the reed of the bagpipes. (Photo, Rudy Nappi / Cover, Simon & Schuster)

NANCY DREW MYSTERY STORIES

The Clue of the Whistling Bagpipes

by CAROLYN KEENE

What Color Is Nancy's Hair?

For twenty years, beginning in 1930, Russell H. Tandy illustrated Nancy Drew as a blonde. But between 1950 and 1980 Nancy's tresses went from golden blond to light blond to red to titian and every tone in between. Fans were extremely confused, and many wrote to the publisher for an explanation. According to illustrator Rudy Nappi, the color production process was responsible for much of this confusion. He began painting Nancy as a blond with a touch of titian, which sometimes darkened in the reproduction process to yellow or red tones. An extreme example of this occurred on the cover of *The Haunted Showboat* (1957), which depicted Nancy as a true redhead.

It seems that Nancy's readers weren't the only ones surprised by the change in Nancy's hair color. In *The Great Detectives* (edited by Otto Penzler, 1978) Harriet S. Adams addressed that period in Nancy's history: "To my consternation an artist had given [Nancy] bright red hair! When I asked why, he told me that the book cover called for three girls. Two were blondes, one a brunette. He felt that a contrast would help the picture."

Rudy Nappi said he was asked to deliberately make Nancy's hair slightly more titian-colored for a brief time after *The Haunted Showboat* debuted in the late 1950s.

Today, Nancy is a reddish blond—in most cases! On the cover of volume #115, *The Nutcracker Ballet Mystery* (1992), she is pure blond. It seems the hair controversy is not over!

Of the more than 150 covers Nappi did, he kept only two paintings, one from the Hardy Boys and one from the Nancy Drew series. Some of his other paintings were sold, but most were simply given away. When an interviewer mentioned how valuable those "lost paintings" are now, Nappi replied, "Yeah, it's crazy. I disliked doing those, yet it's probably more important than anything else I did. I talk about my other work but when I mention the Nancy Drews, people say, 'Really?' "

Rudy Nappi's only regret? "I wish I'd kept the stuff."

1980 to the Present: Debutante Nancy

Between 1979 and 1985, Nancy Drew underwent another major transition. This was the era in which Simon & Schuster introduced new Nancy Drew titles in a paperback format. A flurry of artists, including Ruth Sanderson, Paul Frame, and Glen Hastings, illustrated Nancy during her metamorphosis. Volumes were released under Simon & Schuster's Wanderer, and later Minstrel, imprints. The cover styles reflected the change in publisher and the birth of a new, updated image.

In her paperback debut, volume #57, *The Triple Hoax* (1979), Nancy looked every inch the debutante, peering out thoughtfully toward the reader, her hand poised near her chin. Her hair was decidedly reddish blond, shoulder length with a soft wave. Between the covers, readers found a welcome return to richly detailed illustrations, done in ink with charcoal highlights by Sanderson and Frame. (Many fans were saddened when these wonderful illustrations were dropped from the new texts in the late 1980s. Current paperback editions of the Nancy Drew Mystery Stories have no interior illustrations at all.)

The covers of the new Nancy Drew mysteries now reflect Nancy as a wealthy, privileged sleuth who looks pretty and alert. Her wardrobe runs the gamut from western wear to ball gowns. The backdrops are simple but effective. The colors, and Nancy's facial features, are often so vivid that some of the covers look more like glossy photographs than paintings.

Jim Mathewuse designed this cover for the Nancy Drew Files Case #33, *Danger in Disguise* (1989). (Simon & Schuster)

The Nancy Drew Files, a spin-off series launched in 1986 for the older Nancy Drew fans, are in a cover art category all their own.

The Files covers feature a markedly sexy Nancy, with a handsome young man always lurking in the background. Her clothes often reveal an ample bustline and her expression is mischievous, as if she is privy to a delicious secret. Nancy's aura is one of ultraconfidence: she is the determined career girl destined for greatness. These covers, like the texts, are designed to attract an audience of readers between eleven and fifteen, the ages when girls become increasingly concerned with romance, peer pressure, and forbidden adventure.

One of the current Nancy Drew Files artists is Tricia Zimic of New Jersey, who has tried to keep a level of consistency in the more than fifteen Drew covers she has created. Zimic is responsible for the colorful, upbeat, and highly expressive Nancy Drew that has appeared on *The Cutting Edge*, *Greek Odyssey*, *Rendezvous in Rome*, and other volumes.

Like her predecessors, Zimic uses a live model to help create her vision of Nancy Drew. She takes a photograph of the model, sketches the scene, and then produces the final image on canvas. Zimic says that from "thumbnail sketch to finished painting, the process takes about eleven days."

Under the direction of executive editor Anne Greenberg, along with Simon & Schuster's art director, a number of freelance artists are employed to create covers for the new Nancy Drew Mystery Stories, Nancy Drew Files, and River Heights USA series.

Nancy is continuing through the 1990s with yet another distinctive style. As before, illustrators come and go, trends peak and ebb, spine designs flip back and forth in a bizarre game of artistic Ping-Pong, but Nancy Drew always manages to keep up with the pace.

Tricia Zimic is one of several free-lance artists who design covers for the Nancy Drew mysteries. (Larry Cutchall/© *The Jersey Journal*, 1992)

Remembering Nancy . . . Then and Now

The Essence of Nancy Drew, Supersleuth

"BOY scouts are helpful, kind, faithful, and patriotic. Nancy Drew was 'clever, capable, popular, athletic, unusually pretty, friendly, attractive, skillful, kind, modest, good, brave, poised, keen-minded, plucky, self-reliant, unforgettable, distinctive, forceful, wise, splendid, observant, healthy, responsible, remarkable,' and amazingly . . . normal."

So summarized James P. Jones in his critical analysis for The Journal of Popular Culture (Spring 1973), "Nancy Drew, WASP Supergirl of the 1930s." Nancy can do anything, be anything, achieve anything she desires—and that is certainly one of the reasons she is so popular with her readers and chums alike.

Yet even Mr. Jones's list of Nancy's qualities merely skims the surface of her superpersona. At first glance she seems to be a mere embodiment of impressive talents and traits, but a deeper look shows she is far from a predictable personality. She is a fictional enigma.

Nancy's complex character usually surfaces in dialogue, especially in the early volumes of the series. In The Mystery of the Brass Bound Trunk (1940), for example, a River Heights socialite named Mrs. Joslin demands that Nancy change her plans to go to South America on a trip sponsored by Laurel Leaf Girls' School. It seems that the older woman doesn't want her beautiful, prim daughter Nestrelda mixing with the likes of (horrors!) a detective. Mrs. Joslin concedes that regardless of Nancy's lowly profession, she seems like a reasonable girl who can see how important it is to cancel her cruise reservations immediately. Nancy replies quietly, but firmly, "I am a reasonable person. In fact, I am so reasonable that I believe in justice to myself. I have no intention of giving up the trip."

So emerges the dichotomy of our teen sleuth: reasonable but assertive, altruistic but self-interested, persistent yet courteous, daring yet not entirely reckless, multitalented yet humble. Nancy Drew has all the aggression, impatience, and tenacity of a Type A personality, tempered with the heart of an angel.

Unlike many other children's book heroines, whose personalities often border on the cartoonish, Nancy Drew is not a black-and-white character. And unlike most contemporary sleuths, whose stories are written by one author, many writers (each with his or her own individual style) have contributed to the Nancy Drew books. These factors make any attempt to pin down her character a difficult task.

To complicate matters, Nancy's image has changed quite a bit through the decades. When fans describe what they remember most about Nancy, they are remembering a Nancy Drew of a particular era. Do you recall the sophisticated, golden-haired Nancy, age sixteen, who coolly raced about town in a snappy roadster protecting the interests of the idle rich? Or the eighteen-year-old sleuth of the 1950s, her hair slightly darkened and her convertible in fourth gear, venturing out into the world of international intrigue? Or the Nancy Drew of the 1980s, with reddish blond hair, behind the wheel of her Mustang, somewhat less spirited but more physically active? Or Nancy Drew of today, striving to help the less fortunate yet overly concerned with rock stars, makeup, and how her boyfriend, Ned, is spending his free time?

It is impossible to accurately define Nancy's character because it is so inconsistent and changeable. What hasn't changed, however, are her basic values, her goals, her humility, and her magical gift for having at least nine lives. For more than six decades, her essence has remained intact.

That essence is something fans from every generation can recall with clarity.

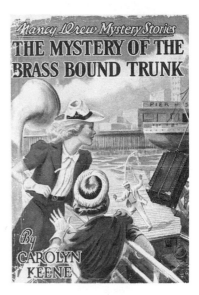

Nancy stands up for herself in *The Mystery of the Brass Bound Trunk* (1940). (Simon & Schuster)

Nancy's Aspirations and Public Image

There has never been any doubt about Nancy's aspirations—she always reaches for the top. The books make frequent references to Nancy's future as a partner in her father's practice, to her winning competitions, to her solving the unsolvable. She perseveres until she reaches her goals and rarely doubts her ability to do so. She is comfortable with her skills and her gender, and assumes she can aspire as high as any of her male counterparts. In the Nancy Drew Files Case #35, *Bad Medicine* (1989), Nancy and Ned are walking through a hospital ward, discussing a current case, when Nancy mentions how fascinating it would be to work in a hospital. In response, Ned tousles his girlfriend's reddish blond hair affectionately and says, "Nurse Nancy, eh?" Nancy quickly replies, "Very funny. I was thinking more about Doctor Drew."

If she ever chose to return to school, Nancy would certainly go the extra mile to get the advanced degree, whether in medicine, law, or teaching. She would only be happy with the ultimate in any field.

Since Nancy Drew can do just about everything well, this works out rather nicely. In *Rascals at Large* (Doubleday, 1971), author Arthur Prager points out, "Police chiefs are forever astounded by [Nancy's] cleverness. When she tries ballet the professionals step back to applaud. Put a paint brush in her hand and watch the praise fly. As to her proficiency with foreign languages, *caramba!*"

"We owe it all to you, Nancy Drew!" is a phrase that appears in many of the volumes. Nancy Drew's achievements routinely make headlines in the River Heights newspapers and often bring her international acclaim. In *The Scarlet Slipper Mystery* (1954), she worked with local and foreign authorities to break up a smuggling ring that involved citizens of the country of Centrovia: "The next day the River Heights *Gazette* and newspapers all over the country featured the story of Nancy Drew and the mystery of the scarlet slipper. The young detective was deluged with telephone calls and wires. One call [from Mrs. Parsons] made her smile broadly. 'Nancy, even if you couldn't dance a step, I would have you in our charity show. Why, my dear, you're the talk of the town!' "

Nancy is a supersleuth, and superteen, in every way. She never fails. One would think this would become irritating, especially to teens who suffer the painful stigma of being unpopular or untalented in their own lives. But Nancy maintains her fans because she is as humble as she is perfect.

In the 1930s, most of Nancy's cases challenged her to locate lost heirlooms for privileged spinsters or track down the rightful inheritances of poor orphans. But by 1950, she was dealing with matters of political and military importance. In the revised version of *The Mystery at Lilac Inn* (1961), she helped locate valuable electronic parts that had been stolen from an American missile base. For that particular piece of detection, she was honored at a special U.S. Army ceremony and presented with the Distinguished Civilian Service Award for her outstanding work.

Nancy takes it all in stride, of course. Her response to such flattery is usually a shy nod, a blush, or a brief speech acknowledging her friends, or the local police, for their help during the case. She always refuses monetary payment for her work, but she graciously accepts gifts from grateful clients. Today, Nancy's memory box is brimming with mementos, awards, and news clippings.

It is clear that Nancy is well equipped emotionally, mentally, and physically to achieve her ultimate goals and fulfill her aspirations. Her supreme confidence (and admirable humility) seem to stem in part from her unusual, charmed upbringing.

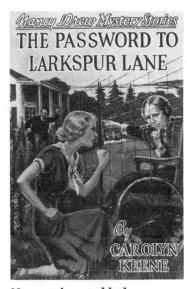

Nancy assists an elderly woman in a wheelchair on the 1933 cover of *The Password to Larkspur Lane.* (Simon & Schuster)

Homespun Values

Overall, Nancy Drew has remained the "good girl" that emerged in the 1930s—a true daughter of America's heartland, complete with the moral code of an educated, privileged, financially secure resident of that region and era. But although the early Nancy remained true to her principles, they didn't stop her from doing anything she wanted to do.

Since her mother died when Nancy was a child, she was forced to take on much of the burden of running the household. This made her more responsible and capable than most of her peers, something the narrator stresses in almost very volume. In *The Mystery of Lilac Inn* (1930), Carson Drew informs Nancy that she needs to find a temporary replacement for housekeeper Hannah Gruen: "Nancy Drew stood for a moment staring blankly at the telephone. She knew that her father, being a man, had no comprehension of the Herculean task which lay before her."

Nancy was aware of the importance as well as the difficulty of her position. "As a famous criminal and mystery-case

Nancy's Memory Box

In many episodes of the Nancy Drew Mystery Stories, grateful recipients of Nancy's sleuthing assistance present her with gifts. Nancy does not accept monetary payment for her work, but she is gracious about accepting mementos from her admirers. What follows is a sampling of the gifts Nancy has received through the decades.

The Crowley mantle clock	From Grace and Allie Horner, to thank Nancy for helping them regain their inheritance. (*The Secret of the Old Clock*, 1930)
A valuable silver urn	From Rosemary and Floretta Turnbull, as a reminder of Nancy's adventure at the Mansion. (*The Hidden Staircase*, 1930)
A bronze medal	From the citizens of Sea Cliff, for Nancy's bravery in saving Bernice Conger from drowning. (*The Whispering Statue*, 1937)
A rare Paul Revere bell	From Mr. Henderson, for Nancy's work in finding a lost relic of antiquity. (*The Mystery of the Tolling Bell*, 1946)
An heirloom cameo ring	From Mrs. Putney, to thank Nancy for finding her jewelry and unraveling the Three Branch swindle. (*The Ghost of Blackwood Hall*, 1948)
A portrait of Nancy herself	From artist Henri Fontaine, for Nancy's great service to the struggling, freedom-loving citizens of Centrovia. (*The Scarlet Slipper Mystery*, 1954)
An aquamarine ring	From Laura Pendleton, as a symbol of her new friendship with Nancy, which began on the water during a storm. (*The Bungalow Mystery*, 1960)
A pin set with tiny diamonds in the shape of a lilac spray	From Emily Crandal and her fiancé, for saving their business and solving *The Mystery at Lilac Inn*. (1961)
Several glossy mink pelts	From Mr. Wells, John Horn, and Chuck Wilson, in remembrance of Nancy's adventure at Big Hill. (*Mystery at the Ski Jump*, 1969)
An Oriental vase	From Lei and Moy Soong to Nancy Drew, for protecting them from the "evil dragons" Ching and Mr. and Mrs. Carr. (*The Clue of the Leaning Chimney*, 1967)
Honorary citizenship in the town of Francisville	From the mayor of Francisville, for banning the ghosts from his town. (*The Clue in the Old Stagecoach*, 1960)

lawyer, Carson Drew found it necessary to maintain a certain social position, and accordingly Nancy was frequently called upon to entertain noted professional men."

If Nancy's upper-class status was at times a heavy burden, it helped make her the strong, capable young woman she was. Her father's income, his expectations, and the unwavering trust he put in his daughter—all paved the way for Nancy to continue her chosen lifestyle.

In *The Lady Investigates* by Patricia Craig and Mary Cadogan (St. Martin's Press, 1981), the authors note, "As a consequence of her ability to uncover crimes, the eighteen-year-old sleuth is largely unrestricted, allowed to board planes at will, take off in pursuit of absolute strangers and even stay out all night. She is subject to none of the minor, irritating pressures of home life and this makes her an object of strong vicarious satisfaction for the juvenile readers."

Nancy is immune to "irritating pressures" to conform in her home life as well as in her crime-fighting methods. Yet these methods are not always above reproach!

Nancy's Selective Respect for Law and Order

In *The Mystery of the Brass Bound Trunk* (1940), Nancy demonstrates "above-reproach" behavior. A man who crashes into Nancy's car gives her one hundred dollars as compensation. When the actual repairs cost only fifty dollars, she decides to find the man and return the balance. To do any less, she feels, would be criminal.

Yet fans also have seen the flip side of Nancy's upstanding behavior. In the series' infancy, she routinely listened to private conversations, sometimes venturing past eavesdropping into blatant spying. She unlocked doors that should have remained locked (breaking and entering) and covertly gathered information from confidential police and corporate records. In these cases, Nancy Drew, number one citizen, bent her own rules to suit her current needs.

In later volumes, her actions conform more to the law. She

"happens" to see a letter that is already opened, or turns a doorknob and finds the door already unlocked. She rarely breaks the law these days, and when she inadvertently does something illegal in her attempts at righting a wrong, she simply chalks it up to altruism. Her reasoning seems to be that it is better for everyone involved, even if she has to bend the law a little, than if she stayed out of the matter entirely.

The Men and Women in Blue

Nancy Drew respects the police but prefers to work alone. In certain cases, however, she must call on the men and women in blue to help her out of a jam.

The local police department, headed up by Nancy's good friend Chief McGinnis, is a visible and important part of the River Heights community. In the original versions of the Nancy Drew Mystery Stories, most of the members of the police force were Irish, with names like Flynn and O'Toole. Once in a while a female police officer appeared, but only if she was in charge of the juvenile division or involved in less taxing cases, such as investigating the theft of rosebushes in Nancy's neighborhood. In current volumes, the officers have lost their Irish brogues, and their methods for apprehending crooks are more realistic than they once were. The detective division is now ethnically mixed, and Detective Penser, in particular, is a great help to Nancy Drew, especially since he is a whiz at breaking codes. In volumes such as #100, *A Secret in Time* (1991), female officers are depicted as capable and active in every branch of police work.

Nancy Drew is on good terms with the local, county, and state police. One of her few confrontations with the law occurs in Nancy Drew Files Case #18, *Circle of Evil* (1987). In that volume, which is wonderfully reminiscent of the theme of the first Nancy Drew books, Nancy is tracking down the burglars who are stealing priceless jewels and artwork from prominent members of the River Heights Country Club. Along the way, she has several verbal sparring matches with rookie cop Detective John Ryan. At one point, when Nancy offers her help and mentions that she is an experienced amateur detective, Ryan replies, "That's fine, Ms. Drew. You keep on solving your own cases and stay away from mine. . . . I warn you, Ms. Drew. Don't mess with this case." Nancy's feelings are hurt, but before the end of the mystery Nancy and Ryan manage to reconcile. The final words of the book illustrate Nancy's sense of humor as well: "Why don't we work together from now on? We might solve more cases. And if it doesn't work out, well, we can always break the truce and start arguing again. Deal, Detective Ryan?" In the end, John Ryan comes across as such an appealing young man that some Nancy Drew fans would like to see Nancy date him in the future!

While the revised texts have updated both the characters and the roles of the police, the original text of volume #1, *The Secret of the Old Clock* (1930), has one of the most memorable police scenes in the series. In it, the county marshal and his deputies are driving at top speed (with Nancy in the lead) in pursuit of a van full of robbers near Moon Lake. " 'Don't fire unless it's necessary,' the marshal ordered his men. 'But if they resist, pepper them!' " The police got their men, and Nancy was later called to testify. It was a dramatic (if a bit cartoonish) climax for Nancy's first official case.

Fears

Nancy's emotions are another important part of her character. The earliest Nancy Drew simply did not feel fear. She had spunk and she had concern, and that was enough. As the series progressed, she became a little more human. She now admits to feeling jealous from time to time; she is obviously fearful when her father's life is in jeopardy, and in one case she actually considers the pain she might suffer if she tries to cross the English Channel in a raft. In Nancy Drew Files Case #3, *Murder on Ice* (1986), she even gives readers a glimpse of a childhood trauma. She pictures herself ice skating, playing Crack the Whip, and suddenly being whipped off the human rope hard and fast. This memory triggers a renewed sense of fear.

Today, Nancy's vulnerability surfaces most often in references to her relationship with Ned Nickerson. In the following passage from Nancy Drew Files Case #9, *False Moves* (1989), for example, Nancy feels a mixture of jealousy and guilt when she learns that Ned is dating someone else:

Well, she admitted silently, she had no one to blame for the breakup with Ned but herself. . . . [W]hen Nancy had been investigating a basketball scandal at Ned's college, she had actually suspected Ned. . . . He had been deeply hurt by her accusation.

Here Nancy shows us another dimension, and that level of vulnerability is a part of the essence of the new Nancy.

Nancy's Nine Lives

The most outstanding component of Nancy Drew's essence is that she has nine lives—actually, more like nine hundred lives! Nancy has been beaten, choked, locked in closets to starve, tied up and deposited in car trunks, pushed into ravines, strangled by snakes, hit on the head by falling theater scenery, and poisoned. She has also spent a good deal of time flying through empty space. Nancy has been known to walk through freight elevator doors to find nothing but air; to step onto the top of a trap door and fall into a dark, dirty dungeon; and to drop off the edge of a mountain without a parachute. And all of these incidents took place in only fifteen random volumes!

Of course, none of these temporary inconveniences ruffle Nancy Drew's steely nerve or deter her from solving her cases. Whatever the odds, whatever the weapon, whatever the obstacle, Nancy rises again, stronger than before, to continue with her mission. But the suspense between the moment of challenge and the moment of victory—*how will she get out of this one?*—has kept fans riveted to these texts for more than sixty years.

What reader can forget the spine-tingling scene in chapter 24 of *The Mystery of the Tolling Bell* (1946) when Nancy, along with Mr. Grumper and crazy Amos Hendrick, was trapped inside a cave? She was at the top of a narrow set of steps, facing the only door to safety, which was locked from the opposite side. Behind her, the tidewater was rushing into the cave. Any second the water was going to rise to the stairs and drown them all. Even if she managed to break down the door she would have been thrust into a room filled with poisonous fumes. Surely Nancy Drew was doomed . . .

Thank goodness Ned Nickerson and George Fayne came to

her rescue in *Tolling Bell*, with the help of a state trooper and a gas mask. But it was a close call. When such scenes are coupled with the gothic overtones so prevalent in the original twenty-five volumes, the threat to Nancy seems even more menacing: Is that mansion she plans to explore truly haunted? What lies at the end of that black tunnel or passageway? Will Nancy survive her mission in the dark forest—or will she meet with a fatal accident, as the gypsy foretold?

In *The Clue in the Crumbling Wall* (1945), Nancy Drew uses her wits to escape from a locked tower. (Simon & Schuster)

When Nancy Drew is working solo she is always well equipped to fight her own battles or to fend off bullies, and when she inadvertently gets her friends in a jam, she keeps her cool and saves the day. In recent volumes of the series, she relies on her martial arts training or whatever sharp object happens to be within reach. In *The Hidden Window Mystery* (1956), for example, Nancy and George are gagged, tied up, and deposited into a hayloft, left to die. But as soon as the coast is clear, Nancy spots a scythe and uses it to saw through her rope bindings. Minutes later, she and George are free.

In the earliest volumes, however, Nancy was not above arming herself with a gun. In *The Hidden Staircase* (1930) Carson gave Nancy permission to stay at the local Turnbull estate for a week. He then went to a locked drawer in his desk, showed her his revolver, and said, "I'll feel better if I know you have it. The Mansion's ghost may turn out to be a livelier one than we expect." Dutifully, Nancy does take the gun when she is ready to leave, telling herself, "And I'll take plenty of ammunition, too! Enough to annihilate an army! Though, truth to tell, I don't know whether I could hit the broad side of a barn or not."

Fortunately, Nancy's prowess with a gun wasn't tested—that time. Readers were left wondering whether she could indeed hit the broad side of a barn. The answer appeared four volumes later in *The Secret at Shadow Ranch* (1931). In that episode, it was ranch owner Mrs. Rawley who urged Nancy, Bess, George, and a young girl named Alice Regor to take a gun with them when they went deep into the Arizona mountains. George laughed and said, "Oh, a bear wouldn't have a ghost of a show if he met four young huskies like us. However, we'll do as you suggest. Nancy can tote the gun because she's the only one who could hit the broad side of a barn!"

In *Shadow Ranch*, Nancy did aim and fire at a large, snarling lynx that was ready to attack: "As the bullet found its mark, there was a terrible crashing in the underbrush, and then all was quiet." George wanted to retrieve the dead animal and bring it home to have it stuffed, but Nancy protested and the lynx was left in its final resting place.

The rules for weaponry have changed drastically for Nancy Drew. Her present publisher states clearly in the writing guidelines that Nancy Drew does not use a gun—ever. Even when Nancy teams up with Joe and Frank Hardy in the Nancy Drew & Hardy Boys SuperMystery series, the boys are allowed to use guns but Nancy is not.

Brains over Brawn

While luck and physical self-defense play an important part in keeping Nancy and friends alive, Nancy most often uses her brains to escape peril. The psychology courses she took in high school have helped her talk several villains out of doing her in, and her mind is quick in a crisis. In *The Clue of the Whistling Bagpipes* (1964), we learn that Nancy has a photographic memory—a handy asset that allows her to make mental pictures of notes, maps, and so on and memorize them, usually before they are stolen or blown to smithereens. The only time that neither Nancy's brawn nor her mental abilities did her much good was in volume #48, *The Crooked Banister* (1971), where she met up with rolling Robbie the robot: "A whirring sound started inside the mechanical man and she turned to face him. The next moment the figure raised his two arms and clasped them tightly around Nancy. He began to squeeze her hard."

Nancy quickly passed out and minutes later, George and Bess found her on the floor beside Mr. Glassboro, who had been the robot's first victim. The only way the cousins were able to stop the robot was to grab a large wrench and whack the mechanical man until his circuits blew and he stopped moving!

Nancy on Wheels

No look at Nancy's endurance would be complete without a discussion of her vehicle. Whether she's driving her snappy

Application for Automobile Insurance

Part of the enjoyment of any hobby is to see the humor in the subject. In the following article reprinted with permission from The Whispered Watchword (April 1993), Nancy Drew fans Kim Aldrich and Nancy Roberts take a not-so-serious look at Nancy Drew's actual, text-documented experiences behind the wheel.

Applicant: *Nancy Drew*   Home Address: *River Heights, USA*   Age: *18*

Date: *April 1, 1949*

List repairs to automobile beginning with earliest damage:

1932—Roadster damaged extensively—repair bill was $20.32!—when applicant was hit by an inexperienced driver at the scene of a fire. Crumpled fender, smashed rear light, bumper dislocated. Bill paid by Baylord Weston.

1934—Applicant dents fender of her roadster and slightly damages paint job on minister's car. Accident occurred while applicant was speeding, supposedly chasing the true mother of twin babies. No claims made on either car.

1937—Applicant claims foreigner in truck backed into borrowed car while pulling out of service station. Bumper torn loose. Bumper and knock in engine repaired; total bill, including two hours of labor, $5. Applicant reimbursed by foreigner muttering about monkey and whispering statue.

1939—Applicant's car was hit at intersection while applicant chased limousine owned by actor Horace St. Will. Driver of other car, Fred Bunce, states that applicant was speeding. Applicant states that Bunce failed to stop at stop sign. Applicant hurriedly left scene of accident.

1940—Applicant's car struck from behind by young man with red hair and mustache and high-pitched voice. Right rear fender crushed. Applicant accepted bribe of $100 (repairs cost only $50) to not call police.

1946—Applicant contends that auto belonging to Ned Nickerson was rammed from behind during storm. Other vehicle allegedly left scene of accident. Applicant's story is unverifiable (of course!) since the supposed occupants of other car, Ferdinand and Amy Slocum and Harry Tyrox, now reside in prison.

1947—Applicant's car needs push to get it back on road. Applicant states that black sedan tried to force her off embankment on lonely road to yacht club. (Note: check with Marine Insurance division since applicant claims her catboat was damaged also.)

1949—Applicant's convertible stolen late at night on lonely road near building with leaning chimney. Since applicant was with boyfriend at time of supposed theft, agent suspects this claim is a variation of the ran-out-of-gas story. Suspicion confirmed when car found later with articles of clothing (shoes) inside.

Evaluation:

At the age of 18, applicant has already had seven accidents and a theft claim. Several accidents occurred when applicant was speeding. Applicant fails to follow sensible driving habits and instead drives at night, during storms, at fire scenes, on lonely roads. Applicant tries to blame other drivers—foreigners, criminals, even a minister! At no time did applicant make a police report, nor did she ever see a doctor. Applicant is a reckless, lying menace.

Disposition: *Application is DENIED.*

Agent: *Kim Aldrich, WALCO Insurance*   Supervisor: *Nancy Roberts*

Reprinted with permission of Nancy Roberts. Originally published in
The Whispered Watchword magazine, 1993.

Nancy's rental car goes off the road in *The Clue of the Whistling Bagpipes* (1964). (Simon & Schuster)

roadster, her convertible, or her current Mustang, Nancy falls victim to foul play. Her cars have been smashed from behind, blown up by dynamite, rear-ended by trucks, and pitched headlong into bodies of water. Because of this, Nancy's cars spend a lot of time at the repair shop. When a car is totaled, her father simply gets her a new one.

Nancy's bad luck with cars extends to those she doesn't even own. In *The Clue of the Whistling Bagpipes* (1964), she rents a sports car to take her to her great-grandmother's estate in Scotland. En route, the rented car goes flying into a river.

Nancy is not always the best driver, regardless of the narrator's descriptions of her motoring skills. But one thing is certain: the image of Nancy Drew dashing about town in search of justice is a vision every Nancy Drew fan remembers with clarity.

Pulitzer Prize–winning novelist Frances Fitzgerald once wrote an article in *Vogue* (May 1980) that stressed the special essence of Nancy's vehicle: "Nancy's car has almost mythical proportions, for, like some magical knightly steed, it will take her anywhere in the imaginary country of River Heights. It gives her total mobility, and while she is driving, a physical equality with men."

Nancy's roadster is as omnipotent as Nancy herself; it is an important part of her image, and part of the essence of the Nancy Drew Mystery Stories.

Now it is time to move on to the more personal parts of Nancy Drew's life and recall the people, places, and things that she encountered while becoming America's number one teen sleuth.

It all begins with Nancy's home . . .

Nancy at Home

At the heart of Nancydrewland is the Drew residence, a large, brick, three-story Colonial house located in the prestigious "Heights" section of the River Heights community. A casual reader could piece together this simple description by skimming a few random volumes, but to determine the actual decor of the home or the daily routine of its occupants requires a bit of sleuthing.

As we saw in chapter 1, most readers view Nancy Drew and her world as fragmented pieces of a puzzle. In one volume a reference to the Drews' sunny veranda may appear; in another a description of Nancy's canopy bed or Carson's garden. Sometimes these references are twenty volumes apart, and considering that many of the Nancy Drew Mystery Stories were revised beginning in 1959, readers have to sift through original and new text versions (and the Nancy Drew Files series) to come up with a complete image. Additional problems arise because of frequent variations in characters and settings. According to former Stratemeyer Syndicate writer Jim Lawrence, "There was supposedly a large file at the syndicate's office; its purpose to keep track of all the places, characters, and things introduced in the Nancy Drew (and other) series. But after seeing the inconsistencies in the books I can only assume that the true purpose of that file was to gather dust!"

Fortunately, readers of this book need not page through more than one hundred volumes to learn about Nancydrewland. What follows is a composite description of Nancy's home and its occupants, based on clues found in books published between 1930 and 1990.

The Setting

Nancy is in her element on the cover of The Clue in the Jewel Box (1943). (Simon & Schuster)

Flanked by rosebushes and stately sycamores, the Drews' home is, at first glance, the very symbol of the upper-middle-class dream. Its circular drive weaves past the house toward a double garage that shelters Nancy's snappy roadster, and later her Mustang; its velvety green lawn leads to a quiet, paved street, properly dotted with similar houses sheltering upstanding citizens. The name of the avenue is never identified, although we do know Park, Vernon, and Center streets are close by, and the upper-level windows of the Drew home offer a panoramic view of scenic farmland. In the distance, "somewhere," lies the bustling city of Chicago.

Warm, balmy evenings find Nancy, lost in thought, on her quaint, white-pillared veranda, perhaps seated beside her father, Carson, who is pondering the latest news in the *River Heights Morning Record*. Their housekeeper, Hannah Gruen, might step outside with an iced pitcher of her finest lemonade and join them for a little chat. A cursory glance by a passerby would reveal nothing unusual about this scenario—unless it was one of *those* days . . .

What did the neighbors think that afternoon the bomb blew up the Drews' mailbox? Or when the mailman, Mr. Ritter, collapsed on the front steps? Surely news spread like wildfire the day that strange van raced by, totaling Nancy's car *and* her boyfriend's—which had both been, unfortunately, parked near the curb. What about the seedy-looking intruders banging at the door and threatening the family, or climbing in the windows to steal evidence (once dashing off with Nancy's lingerie!)? Mrs. Owens, a few doors away, must have raised an incredulous brow seeing Nancy fly overhead in a helicopter, intent on intercepting a burglar climbing up a rickety ladder!

Regardless of the chaos that routinely erupts outside, the decor of the Drew home seems to exude a "quiet elegance." In the morning Nancy often relaxes in the cozy sun-room, propped up against huge pillows on the davenport, sipping a cup of hot chocolate. The living room is a tasteful tableau of rich wooden furniture, overstuffed chairs, a piano, and a large fireplace. The fireplace mantel is the focal point of the room, the spot where

Nancy displays the old clock, the ivory charm, and other mementos she receives from grateful clients. The living room leads to a long hallway, off which are the den and the first-floor library. The den is the informal family gathering place, a hideaway where Nancy and Ned sip sodas and watch old Laurel and Hardy movies or steal a tender kiss. The library is Carson's personal retreat after a long day at the law office. It is lined with bookcases and features a large desk and tufted leather chair. The spacious kitchen is pink and white, complete with a breakfast nook and the latest top-of-the-line appliances. In 1930, housekeeper Hannah Gruen had an electric refrigerator (not a mere icebox), and now she has a microwave oven and a dishwasher. The Donna Reed of the Drew home, Hannah is forever preparing special dishes that fill the house with mouth-watering aromas, adding to the warm, inviting atmosphere.

The second story has at least five bedrooms, one each for Nancy, Carson, and Hannah, along with guests' quarters and Hannah's sewing room. There's even a second study for Nancy's late-night attempts at decoding old ledgers.

Nancy Drew's room is golden yellow and white, with a large four-poster bed, crisp cotton curtains and spreads, a desk, and deep, plush carpeting. She has her own bathroom and dressing table. In recent books in the series a special dresser was added, the ideal place to keep her jewelry and mementos from her numerous cases. In the 1980s she acquired an elaborate stereo system, color television, telephone, and answering machine of her own. Her closets spill over with every manner of clothing: heavy down jackets for ski-trip murder mysteries, casual slacks and blouses for investigating local arson cases, and jewel-studded gowns for special evenings at the River Heights Country Club. It is the perfect room for the perfect sleuth and the perfect daughter.

Climbing the stairs to the third story, we find a large attic and extra storage rooms to hold dusty family heirlooms, old furniture, and Nancy's mementos from grammar school.

Even the family dog has his own little domain—the recreation room downstairs in the finished cellar.

Although the Drew residence has changed slightly over the decades, it has always remained Nancy's haven of comfort and security, a place in which to mull over a problem, trade wits with Dad, share cozy chats with chums Bess and George, or bring in orphans for some much-needed TLC.

Carson Drew gives Nancy advice in *The Secret in the Old Attic* (1970). (Simon & Schuster)

Most of all, it is the place where the people she loves are just a hug away.

Illustrious Carson Drew

As Betsy Caprio wrote in *The Mystery of Nancy Drew*, "Any reader's wish to find a perfect father is certainly more than satisfied by Carson Drew. He is all a dad could be: affirming, devoted, affectionate, concerned and generous." He is also endowed with the patience of a saint and a substantial yearly income—two essentials for surviving life with his spirited, world-traveling daughter.

Like the other characters in the series, Carson has undergone a multitude of changes. In *The Secret of the Old Clock* (1930), fans were first introduced to Nancy's father, a noted criminal- and mystery-case lawyer, "known far and wide for his work as a former district attorney." When Nancy bursts into the room, raving about the injustice of the late Josiah Crowley's will, Carson looks up from his newspaper (he always has a newspaper nearby) and gives her his respectful attention, pondering "the rich glow of the study lamp upon Nancy's curly golden bob. Not at all the sort of head which one expected to indulge in serious thoughts."

Yet Carson was proud of those serious thoughts, and from that day on he supported her attempts at righting the world's wrongs and expanding her intellectual horizons.

The original Carson was notably older and more mild-mannered than the Carson of the 1990s. In the 1930s he wore horn-rimmed spectacles, smoked cigars, and carried a cane. To relax, he tended his rose garden and radish beds or took a leisurely walk to the nearby park. He usually preferred Nancy to address him as Father, rather than Dad. He was strict about making sure Nancy telephoned if she was going to be even a tad late, and he insisted she bring a respectable adult companion along on her out-of-state adventures. He also spent a good portion of his time spouting fatherly advice.

By 1940 Carson was tall, dignified, and known across the

United States as a "fighter" who took on the most difficult legal challenges without backing down from his convictions. He automatically called upon Nancy to help with his cases and assumed she would be able to solve mysteries with efficiency and ingenuity. He respected her intuition and didn't even blink an eye when Nancy volunteered his professional services to clients who hadn't a dime to pay his legal fees.

Post–World War II Carson was tall and handsome, endowed with good humor and a less formal set of clothes. By 1990 he is described as a distinguished, good-looking man in his forties, with dark hair that is flecked with gray at the temples. His cases are now laced with international intrigue, and his office is completely computerized.

However, it was long before the 1990s that Carson realized it was best not to argue with Nancy when she had a particular goal in mind, even if his own instincts advised caution: "You're a peach, Father. You let me do anything I like and never make fun of my wild ideas," chimed Nancy in *The Clue of the Broken Locket* (1934). Perhaps Carson's leniency with his daughter was at times unrealistic, but he, like everyone else in Nancy's life, could not remain immune to her charm and undaunted enthusiasm.

Through time we can piece together details of Carson's background. He was widowed when Nancy was three years old (in early volumes she was ten when her mother died) and no other woman has quite measured up to his wife—at least not enough to prompt him to remarry. His alma mater is Hale University, where he enjoyed an active social life, studied geology, and played a mean game of tackle football. (One reason he is so fond of Ned Nickerson is because of their mutual athletic prowess.) The youthful Carson reveled in earning his law degree and became a traditional, upwardly mobile man—a yuppie of the late 1800s.

As for Carson's family, his parents are rarely mentioned (although in one instance Nancy recalls her grandfather "fondly"). Carson does have a "spinster" sister named Eloise, a tall, attractive woman who lives in New York City in a stately brownstone apartment. She is employed as a teacher at a Manhattan girls' school and is a great aficionado of the theater. Aunt Eloise crops up throughout the series as the perfect relative for Nancy to visit when her cases take her to the East Coast.

Aunt "Lou" is right behind Nancy when she investigates a mink fur scam in *The Mystery at the Ski Jump* (1952) and when she's hot on the trail of the robber of the fifty-thousand-dollar dragon vase in *The Clue of the Leaning Chimney* (1949). The books reveal that Nancy closely resembles Eloise, and that when Carson was first widowed, Aunt Eloise almost left her career to rear Nancy—until Hannah Gruen found the Drews and Aunt Eloise was able to stay in New York.

Mention of Carson's other relatives is scarce, shedding little light on his heritage. One cousin, Susan Carr of Charlottesville, Virginia, came in handy during *The Hidden Window Mystery* (1956). It is unclear, however, whether she is a cousin of Carson's or of Nancy's deceased mother. Readers must use their imaginations to fill in the missing pieces of Carson's past.

The most striking element of Carson Drew's character is the intricate, deep relationship he develops with his only daughter. He indulges her but is careful not to spoil her. He is free with his compliments, ever beaming about her common sense and uncanny ability to solve a mystery. He is her staunchest supporter when she wants to go the extra mile to solve a particularly complex case. That "extra mile" often turns into hundreds of miles as Nancy routinely asks for permission to scurry off to places like New York, Canada, and Louisiana. Still, Carson honestly seems to delight in the excitement Nancy brings him—even when that excitement threatens his own life. On a deeper level, father and daughter share a special emotional bond, and although both remain cool and controlled about the life-threatening perils of "others," they are absolute mushmelons when either one of them is in danger.

During a memorable scene in *The Hidden Staircase* (1930), for example, Carson falls victim to one of the meanest villains in the series, Nathan Gombet. Carson is lured to a remote Gothic estate, locked in a room, and tied up with rope. His only meal is stale bread and water, and eventually he is left in the cold room to starve until he gives in to Nathan's demand for twenty thousand dollars. Carson's situation is perilous enough, but it worsens when Nathan threatens to kidnap Nancy as well: "A look of horror came into Mr. Drew's eyes." His only thoughts are of Nancy, whom he hopes is safely at the home of the elderly Turnbull sisters:

*"I wonder if Nancy is still there!" flashed through his mind. "Oh, if
only she returns to River Heights before that fiend gets his hands on her!"
It was characteristic of Carson Drew to think of his daughter's safety before his own. She was always first.*

Nancy's feelings about her father are just as strong. The only
thing that can really move her to tears is the fear that her father
is in peril, or worse, that she might not ever see him again. She
is also fierce in her protection of his reputation and honor, and
in cases where someone demeans him, she turns into a wild-
cat—her tone becomes brassy and cutting.

At times, their close relationship (and Nancy's possessiveness) moves toward extremes. In Nancy Drew Files Case #28
The Black Widow (1988), Carson falls in love with beautiful Nina
da Silva. Nancy becomes so jealous that her behavior borders
on the irrational, but Carson is smitten and he can't see past
Nina's facade. Soon, chaos erupts en route to Rio. This is one of
the rare times that Carson and Nancy are at odds—and both of
them suffer from the impact before it is resolved.

It may strike readers as unusual that an eligible man like
Carson Drew doesn't have a more active social life, but then
again, he doesn't seem to have much luck in the area of romance. In *Mystery of the Glowing Eye* (1974), he employed a female
assistant named Marty King, who attempted to interfere with
Nancy's sleuthing activities while blatantly pursuing dear old
Dad. Additional problems arose with Marty because Carson
soon "began to realize that she was always arranging my business affairs so that she and I would have to eat luncheon or dinner together." And when Carson saw how viciously jealous
Marty was of Nancy, the situation worsened. In the end Carson
asked Marty to leave because she asked him to marry her.
Nancy's response was typical: " 'Dad,' she said, 'if you ever
want to find me a new mother, please promise me she won't be
someone who tries to solve my mysteries!' Her father laughed
heartily. 'I promise,' he said."

Carson and Nancy have had their misunderstandings
through the years, but they continue to share a healthy, virtually
idyllic father-daughter relationship that flourishes and deepens
with each mystery. Carson admitted once that his secret dream
was to hang a shingle "Carson Drew & Daughter" over his law
office door—and who knows? If Nancy ever decides to break
down and attend college, his dream may come true.

Nancy's Lost Mother: A Key to Nancy's Lineage

It is extremely common in girls' series books to have an orphaned or half-orphaned heroine. As collector Nancy Roberts pointed out in an analysis of this phenomenon in *The Whispered Watchword* magazine, mothers are fifty percent more expendable than fathers. Without a mother in the picture, sleuths like Nancy Drew have a lot more freedom of movement. In Nancy's case she also takes on the dual role of daughter/surrogate wife for Carson, and this in turn provides her with the charmed status of being a carefree teen with adult liberties. Nancy Drew is a strange breed of girl/woman—which always works to her advantage.

But what happened to Mrs. Drew?

We know very little about Nancy's deceased mother. Clues are few and far between in the series, and those provided sometimes contradict each other. Mrs. Drew died when Nancy was three from "a sudden illness," but that illness is never explained. The books state numerous times that Nancy looked a great deal like her mother, but this tells us little; there are even more references to Nancy Drew resembling her Aunt Eloise, who is *Carson's* sister.

Mrs. Drew is mentioned indirectly in the original volume of *The Hidden Window Mystery* (1956). Housekeeper Hannah brings down a bunch of peacock feathers that had been stored for years in the attic and announces they had belonged to Nancy's maternal grandmother, Mrs. Austin. Therefore, we know that Mrs. Drew's maiden name was Austin.

The Clue of the Whistling Bagpipes (1964) treats us to a bounty of information about Nancy's roots, and fans were surely delighted (but not surprised) to learn that Nancy and her mother had blue blood running through their veins! In *Bagpipes*, the Drews receive a letter from Nancy's great-grandmother, Lady Douglas, of Inverness-shire, Scotland. She informs Carson that she intends to turn over her large estate to the National Trust of Scotland and needs some of her relatives to sign releases before the transaction can be completed. Nancy will also inherit something from the estate: a priceless brooch with a large center topaz surrounded by diamonds. This correspondence leads to a full range of adventures in Scotland for Nancy, who gets the chance to enjoy the benefits of her genealogical connections.

In the course of the story Nancy finally meets her great-grandmother, Lady Douglas, face to face. Lady Douglas is the widow of a former member of the House of Lords, in one of Scotland's first families.

Douglas House is a huge estate located in the Highlands surrounded by sycamore, beech, and birch trees. It is decorated with rare antiques, elaborate rugs, and vintage portraits of Nancy's ancestors. Great-grandma is a "slender, frail, white-haired woman with a beautiful face and a distinguished mien." It is also mentioned that Nancy's great-great-grandmother was a Cameron, thereby providing enough information to chart five generations of Nancy Drew's Scottish heritage.

How Nancy's mother died, the circumstances surrounding her courtship with Nancy's father, and how Miss Austin migrated to America remain a mystery.

In *The Clue of the Whistling Bagpipes*, Nancy Drew traces her Scottish heritage back to the Douglas family, whose crest is shown here.

Hannah Gruen

In doing away with Nancy's mother, it no doubt became obvious to Edward Stratemeyer when he created the Nancy Drew series that someone else had to tend to domestic duties in that large, busy house. Hannah Gruen materialized to fill the role.

In the early books, Hannah was an elderly servant, a "maid-of-all work" who cooked and cleaned for the Drew family. She had little dialogue and neither Nancy nor Carson confided in her. Hannah was always referred to as Mrs. Gruen, but of her marriage or widowhood we know nothing more.

At first, her presence in the Drew home was strictly professional. She addressed Nancy with the formal "Miss Nancy" and routinely took directions from Nancy concerning the preparation of dinners and how to keep everything in shape for unexpected guests—or intruders. She quickly became a whiz at packing for Nancy at a moment's notice, especially for international trips that required steamer trunks of gear.

Nancy's
Noble Scottish Ancestry

Lady Cameron of Scotland
(her great, great maternal grandmother)

◆

Lady Douglas
(her great grandmother)

◆

Mrs. Austin
(her grandmother)

◆

Miss Austin – Wife of Carson Drew
(her mother)

◆

Nancy Drew

Designed especially for **The Nancy Drew Scrapbook**
by Nancy Drew fan, Marge Romano

Of all the characters in the series, Hannah was the one whose strong midwestern speech patterns were most pronounced. Phrases like "Land sakes, Nancy, there's so much commotion in this house a body can't even think!" (*The Clue of the Tapping Heels,* 1939) gave regional flavor to the stories.

Hannah was born and raised in the area of River Heights and had a sister living nearby who would sometimes accompany Hannah to "moving picture shows." Later in the series, readers found out that she had a number of cousins as well, including Mrs. Bealing, a housekeeper in a neighboring home.

The Quest of the Missing Map (1942) tells us how Hannah found her way to the Drews. It unfolds that she was formerly employed by the Smiths, "once a wealthy River Heights family," who had returned from a trip around the world facing serious financial straits. Their daughter Ellen (who eventually becomes entrenched in Nancy's current case) was promptly assigned the drudgery of household duties.

As it turns out, Mrs. Drew's life and Hannah Gruen's employment with the Smiths terminated simultaneously. Hannah began working for the Drews on a temporary basis, but they were so pleased with her work they kept her on.

By the mid-1940s, Hannah's place in the household had reached a new level. In *The Mystery of the Tolling Bell* (1946), the narrator introduced her as "Mrs. Gruen, the family housekeeper, whom [Nancy] regarded almost as a parent. . . . Because Nancy was unusually sensible, clever and talented, Mrs. Gruen allowed her a great deal of freedom." When *The Crooked Banister* rolled off the presses in 1971, Hannah was described as a lovable woman, a pleasant-faced housekeeper whom the family relied on to keep the house running. Hannah's age bounced from elderly to middle-aged and back again between volumes 1 and 56, but one thing never wavered—she is the best cook in River Heights. Her specialties include waffles, roast chicken, and apple pie with lots of cinnamon.

Hannah is an efficient woman, obviously fond of her employers, and as the series progressed, she took a more active role in family matters and in Nancy's adventures. The more she became involved with the adventures, the more she needed time to relax and recuperate. She began crocheting with a vengeance at one point, and she tends her rose garden on particularly unnerving days.

Hannah Gruen's primary purpose in the series is to play the role of the worrywart. Since she is not really Nancy's mother this does not come across as smothering, but instead as fretful, concern. Her reactions to Nancy's escapades, and the stream of strangers dashing in and out of the house, provide much-needed comic relief on many occasions. It's interesting to note that Hannah becomes most upset not by the bevy of burglars who find their way into her life, but instead by the problematic kittens, wild minks, screeching birds, live chickens, and squirming lobsters that cross her path in the course of Nancy's adventures. Her bone of contention is the family pet, Togo, who constantly upsets her daily routine.

Hannah Gruen helps out in *The Kachina Doll Mystery* (1981). (Simon & Schuster)

Most of the time Hannah is calm and serene, happily dishing up creamed chicken and ironing Carson's shirts, and her carrying-on is usually restricted to a well-meaning "*Please* be careful, Nancy"—unless Carson or Nancy is unjustly attacked. For example, in *Nancy's Mysterious Letter* (1932) Hannah unleashed her wrath when snippety Mrs. Sheets arrived to accuse Nancy of stealing a letter and the money that was in it. Hannah was outraged at the thought of Nancy being accused of stealing, and let Mrs. Sheets hear about it: " 'If you don't keep a civil tongue in your head, Missus, I'll get the cops myself, so I will,' Hannah fumed. 'Or I'll lay the broad side of the broom against that impudent face of yours!' "

Fortunately, Nancy calmed Hannah down before the broom hit its mark.

Whenever Hannah has to leave to visit relatives or go on holiday, she is temporarily replaced by Effie, once described as "a willing but somewhat stupid maid who often did a day's work for the Drews." Effie is a poor substitute for efficient Hannah Gruen, but she means well and the Drews try to retain their patience until dear Hannah arrives home.

Today, Hannah is a pleasant, gray-haired woman in her midsixties, with expressive, soft brown eyes and a caring temperament. She is accepted as a full-fledged member of the Drew family. Both Carson and Nancy have said that they just couldn't imagine their lives without Hannah.

And neither could we.

Togo the Terrier

The fourth member of the Drew household is Togo, the dog. In true Drew form, he has gone through a number of breed changes since his creation, and his temperament is as changeable as his pedigree. At times Nancy, and especially Mrs. Gruen, are not certain whether to caress him lovingly or relegate him to the nearest pound on the grounds of canine mischief. Togo is indeed as unique as his masters.

Togo first appeared in the original text of *The Whispering Statue* (1937); he began trailing Nancy when she, Bess, and George were attending the opening ceremonies of nearby Harrison

Nancy Drew deals with a mischievous Togo in The Hidden Window Mystery (1956). (Simon & Schuster)

Park. No matter what Nancy and her friends did, the dog continued to follow them about—wreaking havoc everywhere he went. He was initially described as a frisky bullterrier with a well-shaped head; "a thorobread of high calibre" who "cast a wistful eye at every flower-bed they passed." Nancy soon became attached to him and decided to bring him home until she could find his owner.

It was Bess who finally named him: " 'I wish we knew his name,' Bess remarked. 'We might call him Togo.' " And so they did.

Togo was thoroughly enamored of Nancy, to the point that he doggedly followed her on a train to Sea Cliff in *The Whispering Statue* (1937). Needless to say, Togo's owners never did surface and Nancy acquired a loyal pet.

Togo pops in and out of the Nancy Drew Mystery Stories at random—sometimes intercepting lost evidence, but most of the time stealing it for his own amusement. In *The Clue of the Whistling Bagpipes* (1964) he makes a short comeback, but is reincarnated as a Scotch terrier, bearing little resemblance to the original Togo. In *The Hidden Window Mystery* (1956), he helped Nancy search for lost letters that the mailman had dropped near the Drew home and became the hero of the day when he found the corner of an envelope with the missing address. That evening, the pup was treated to Mrs. Gruen's roast leftovers.

One of the more touching scenes with Togo occurs in *Mystery at the Ski Jump* (1952). Nancy was both puzzled and concerned because so many unsuspecting victims were being misled into buying worthless stock in a fur company. Her father was away on a business trip when she sorely needed his advice. Leading Togo to her father's study, Nancy stared somewhat sadly into the deserted room: " 'I love this room, Togo,' Nancy confided. 'It makes me feel so close to Dad. Let's pretend he's here, shall we?' " At this point she called upon Togo to play the role of "Dad" in their conference. Togo complied, barking and frolicking in grand style.

Whatever his breed, Togo always proves to be a great comfort to Nancy in times of turmoil. He is the perfect furry addition to the Drew home.

And so the stage is set. Let us move on to the many places and personalities of rambling River Heights.

The City of River Heights

Many of Nancy's most exciting adventures take place in her hometown—and for good reason. It is a mythical metropolis perfectly suited to a sleuth's needs. In *The Secrets of the Stratemeyer Syndicate* (Ungar, 1986), Carol Billman discusses the important role River Heights plays in the series: "In one respect, it functions like Alice's aboveground world in Lewis Carroll's fantasy or Dorothy's home base, Kansas, in *The Wonderful Wizard of Oz*. . . . There is, however, an important distinction. Nancy has everything she needs in River Heights: security, independence, approbation, and mystery. She does not need a Wonderland or Emerald City."

The allure of River Heights is strong; its people and places reach out from the pages of the books to capture readers' interest and imagination. The only drawback of River Heights is its elusiveness in the real world. In Linda Sunshine's book, *The Memoirs of Bambi Goldbloom* (Simon & Schuster, 1987), the title character, Bambi, compares her own life to Nancy Drew's: "Everywhere she turned, Nancy would stumble over hidden staircases, mysterious letters, broken lockets, haunted attics, secret diaries or unclaimed signet rings. . . . It was frustrating for me to compare my mundane life to Nancy's. . . . Let's face it, Hohokus [New Jersey] was no River Heights."

This illustration by Russell Tandy from *The Mystery at Lilac Inn* (1930) offers a rare glimpse of the River Heights business district. (Simon & Schuster)

River Heights: Metropolis

River Heights has evolved from a small, quiet town in the early Nancy Drew books to a thriving metropolis. Through the decades, Carolyn Keene has added new streets, business establishments, and parks as the stories required them, along with airports and train stations to help Nancy and her friends travel to and from the city. Careful study of the volumes published from 1930 to 1993 allows us a glimpse into River Heights, then and now.

When Nancy steps out of her cozy, three-story residence, she can easily walk the few blocks to the homes of her pals Bess, George, and Helen, then take a stroll to nearby Walden Park. If she so desires, she can stop at Jackson's Pharmacy for an ice-cream soda, then travel west to Park Street, into the River Heights business district.

River Heights proper is divided by the great Muskoka River, over which the county officials erected a formidable railroad bridge. River Road runs the length of that waterway, leading to outlying Masonville, Cliffwood, Welding, Winslow, and Ned Nickerson's hometown of Mapleton.

In the original texts of the Nancy Drew Mystery Stories, a fine line existed between the prestigious, residential "Heights" area, the business center, and the "other side" of town (located, of course, on the wrong side of the tracks). There, the rows of abandoned warehouses and peculiar thrift shops were fairly hopping with intrigue. Only through descriptions of the southern regions of River Heights were readers given any sign that the Great Depression, or the influx of struggling immigrants during that period, had any part in Nancy's world at all. *The Mystery at Lilac Inn* (1930) gave us a vivid picture of the section known as Dockville:

> Nancy drove toward the river, zigzagging her way from one street to another. The pavement was poor, and as she approached the slum district it became even more bumpy. . . . She was confronted with row upon row of tenement houses, all alike and of a dingy and uninviting appearance. Swarms of dirty children were playing in the streets.

Soon after this observation, Nancy quickly left Dockville, expressing her disgust and fear of the area.

Near Dockville, and scattered throughout the city, were an inordinate number of fraudulent fortune-tellers and palm readers. River Heights was overflowing with all manner of "undesirables," who, according to Hannah Gruen, included struggling actors, gypsies, and low-ranking domestic workers. These characters routinely rented space on both Main Street and Clayton Avenue, right beside the more fortunate jewelry dealers, judges, estate managers, and French boutiques.

Recent titles in the Nancy Drew series greatly downplay the number, and character traits, of River Heights undesirables. In the 1930s and 1940s the majority of the poor residents, criminals, and gypsies were either foreign or "colored," with slovenly habits and less-than-noble motivations. In the mid-1950s, Harriet S. Adams began to delete all racist references from revised editions of the series. Such stereotypes no longer appear in the volumes.

Descriptions of the "wrong side of the tracks" are also more realistic these days. Poverty-stricken communities are no longer presented merely as a thorn in River Heights' side, but as places and people that are victims of a bad economy. The revised texts are free of references to the world wars, the Depression, and the Communist threat.

Schools, Sports, and Entertainment

Although the city has a wonderful public school system, many Heights social climbers send their offspring to private institutions such as Laurel Leaf Girls' School. For special lessons they attend Blackstone Music College, Master Mastrovani's singing school, Señor Roberto's Trick Riding Academy, and Madame Dugrand's ballet academy. In volume #110, *The Nutcracker Ballet Mystery* (1992), Bess, George, and Nancy solve a case at Madame's academy and end the season with a gala production of *The Nutcracker Suite*.

Sports are popular among River Heights residents, so the baseball fields, bicycle paths, and parks are usually crowded. At the gala opening ceremonies of Harrison Park, not far from Bess Marvin's house, Nancy encountered her first clue for *The Whispering Statue* (1937) and, you will recall, found her terrier, Togo. The park spans many acres and contains a small lake. It has an arched entrance gate, beautiful gardens blooming with larkspurs and roses, and a small pavilion for entertainment.

Nancy protects a young boy when the circus comes to town in *The Mystery of the Ivory Charm* (1936). (Simon & Schuster)

Nancy frequents Harrison, and other parks, for quiet moments to ponder her mysteries.

Every year the circus comes to town, bringing with it the excitement of the big top and the daring stunts of acrobats. Yet try as she might, Nancy just can't seem to enjoy the festivities without meeting danger. In *The Mystery of the Ivory Charm* (1936), Nancy was called upon to save the little elephant boy, Coya, from a brutal whipping by his guardian, Rai. Shortly thereafter a "huge jungle snake" wrapped its powerful coils about her "in a venomous grip of death." Naturally, Nancy survived, Coya was declared a lost rajah of India by chapter 20, and Nancy added a beautiful ivory charm to her cache of mementos.

Years later, in *The Ringmaster's Secret* (1953), the traveling Sim's Circus was the setting for Bess Marvin's favorite mystery. Not only did Nancy save the day for lovely aerialist Lolita and her betrothed, Pietro, but she also made her own debut as a trick bareback rider. During the final scene, all gathered at the big tent for a wedding reception and a command performance. It was the most memorable circus in River Heights history!

Meeting Community Needs

Ever conscious of civic responsibility, River Heights has its own foundling home, nursing home, day-care center, and civic league, as well as a retirement community, Climson Oaks, located on Wilson Avenue. There are two hospitals, an efficient fire department, a vast municipal center, and a top-notch police force. Plenty of banks dot the business district, ready to hold the savings of heiresses and the newly acquired wealth of orphans, and as River Heights approached the nineties, cash machines became commonplace.

For special dances, fund-raisers, and power lunches, the site of choice is the River Heights Country Club. Citizens with less prestige settle for fast food at Frank's Pizza, followed by a matinee at the Grand Cinema.

The *River Heights Morning Record* keeps everyone abreast of the latest gossip, often including the news of Nancy and her latest accomplishments.

The Ever-Changing Topography of River Heights

Nancy's hometown changes its topography with each new volume of the Nancy Drew Mystery Stories, and since 1989, when Simon & Schuster published the spin-off series, River Heights USA, the city has grown by leaps and bounds.

The River Heights series focuses on Nancy Drew's next-door neighbor, Nikki Masters, a junior at River Heights High School, with cameo appearances by Nancy Drew, Bess Marvin, and George Fayne. Nikki has shiny blond hair and blue eyes just like Nancy, but while Nancy drives a blue Mustang, Nikki zips through town in a metallic blue Camaro.

Nikki and her friends Robin Fisher, Lacy Dupree, and Tim Cooper (along with Nikki's archrivals Brittany Tate and Jeremy "Preppy" Pratt) frequent sites introduced in the original Nancy Drew texts, including Moon Lake, the Pizza Palace, and the River Heights Mall. But author Carolyn Keene has also created new places that the teens of the River Heights series can call their own. In volume #12, *Hard to Handle* (1991), readers learn about Café Chow, a "romantic college hangout" where the high schoolers have dinner on special dates; the more informal after-school eatery called The Loft; and Leon's, which serves up the best ice cream in town.

But where exactly *is* River Heights?

Mildred Wirt Benson said that when she wrote the early volumes she pictured River Heights in Iowa, and this idea is supported with descriptions of vast farmland, cornfields, and references to Nancy as a true child of the Midwest. In *Nancy's Mysterious Letter* (1932), we learn that Emerson College, where Ned is captain of the football team, is located on a tributary of the "mighty Ohio River." (Although this particular volume was written by Walter Karig, he maintained Mildred Benson's preference for the midwestern flair of River Heights.) In other volumes, however, Carson Drew makes frequent trips "west" to

Chicago, making Indiana and even Ohio other possible locations.

To complicate matters, when Harriet Adams began revising the series in the late 1950s, River Heights took on an unmistakably eastern ambience. It began to look like New Jersey, the location of the Stratemeyer Syndicate offices. The characters' midwestern phrases were replaced with less distinctive speech patterns. New York was just a step away, and in *The Sky Phantom* (1976), Nancy takes a vacation to a special flying school "out in the Midwest," making it sound as if a trip there was a major event.

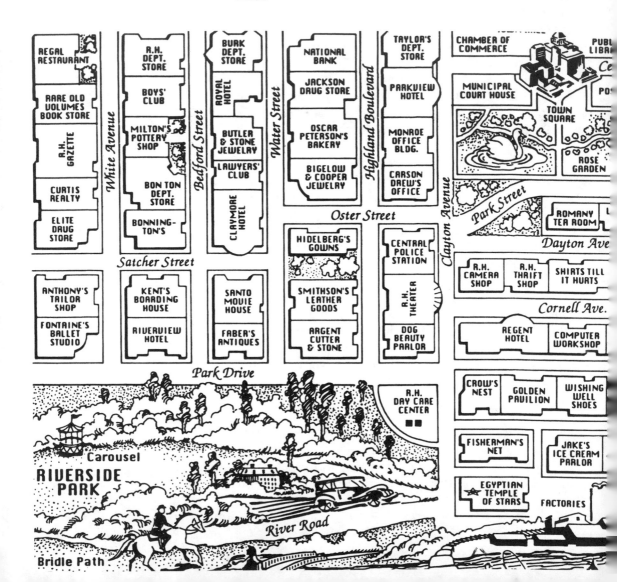

In her book *The Mystery of Nancy Drew*, Betsy Caprio proposes that River Heights is in Holmes County, Ohio. By analyzing clues from the books and interviewing Nancy Drew authors, Caprio developed a map of River Heights, a portion of which appears on pages 86–87. However, the present writers' guidelines for the Nancy Drew Files state that River Heights is now a suburb of Chicago.

The debates continue. . . .

Wherever River Heights is located on the U.S. map, it has all the qualities a young sleuth could hope for. No wonder Nancy can't wait to come home after her journeys to faraway places.

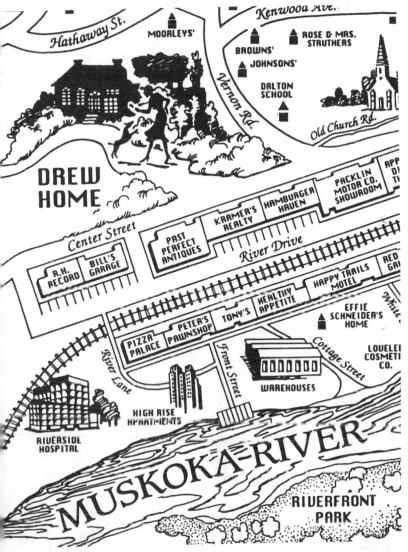

This portion of a map of River Heights, designed by Betsy Caprio for her book *The Mystery of Nancy Drew: Girl Sleuth on the Couch*, shows the town's main streets, businesses, and government buildings that surround the Drew home. (Source Books, Inc.)

Parks and Community Centers

Harrison Park
Walden Park
Riverfront Park
River Heights Civic Center
River Heights Day-Care Center
The River Heights Community Theatre

Eateries

The Red Lion Tea Room ● The Pizza Palace ● River Heights Cafe
The Regal ● Jake's Ice Cream Parlor
The Romany Tea Room

Hotels

The Claymore
The Riverview

Newspapers

River Heights Morning Record
River Heights Gazette

Livery

The Gold Star Cab Company

Movie Theaters

The Grand Cinema
Santo Movie

Mass Transit

River Heights Railroad Station
River Heights Airport

Schools

River Heights High School ● Pineview School
The Brewster Academy ● Laurel Leaf Girls' School
Blackstone Music College ● Riverview College

Hospitals

Rosemont Hospital
River Heights General

Shops and Department Stores

Burk's
Hidelberg's
Taylor's
The River Heights Mall
Smithson's Leather Goods
Butler & Stone Jewelers
Wishing Well Shoes

Nancy's Chums: Partners in Fighting Crime

In spite of her independent spirit, Nancy Drew enjoys company while tracking down dastardly villains. Since the police rarely get involved in her cases until the resolution (when Nancy gets most of the credit), she often calls upon her friends to help her out. Occasionally she phones them to ask for help, but more often than not they all happen to be socializing when catastrophe strikes. Whether you're en route to a square dance, skiing in Canada, sightseeing in South America, or dining at a quaint inn, life is never boring when you're pals with Nancy Drew.

Nancy Drew (right) and her chums Bess and George dig for clues in *The Mystery of the Moss-Covered Mansion* (1941). (Simon & Schuster)

Helen Corning

Helen Corning was Nancy's first accomplice, introduced in the 1930 version of *The Secret of the Old Clock* as "a particular chum of Nancy's" who had attended school (presumably high school) with the then-fledgling sleuth and had graduated three years before Nancy.

Helen is depicted as a typical River Heights teen, a pretty brunette with a shapely figure and pleasant smile. Her life is filled with parties, summer vacations, social climbing, and pursuit of the perfect mate. In *The Hidden Staircase* (1959), Helen's ultimate dream came true: she informed Nancy she was engaged to Jim Archer, who worked for the Tristam Oil Company. (Jim Archer is Helen's fiancé in the revised texts of the series, but in the original text version of *Nancy's Mysterious Letter* [1932] she arrived at a college party with her date, Buck Rodman.) Nancy was polite throughout Helen's description of the wedding plans and the couple's dreams for the future, but as always, she was more concerned with her current case than with lavender frills on bridesmaids' gowns.

Helen and Nancy behave more like acquaintances than bosom buddies. They both enjoy a good tennis match, lunch at a local restaurant, and swapping tips for keeping the servants in line, but Helen's major task is to act as a plot device to help Nancy achieve her current goal.

In *The Secret of the Old Clock* (1930), for example, Helen provided Nancy with tickets to the local fund-raiser, which Nancy used as an excuse to get into the Tophams' estate and get a peek at the infamous mantel clock. One of Helen's relatives also ran Camp Avondale at Moon Lake, conveniently located near a row of bungalows brimming with seedy characters.

In *The Hidden Staircase* (1959) we are introduced to Helen's great-aunt Rosemary Hayes and her great-grandmother "Miss Flora" Turnbull, who reside in a marvelous haunted estate called Twin Elms. One of Helen's uncles owns a retail store that plays a role in another of Nancy's mysteries. Generally speaking, Helen's relatives are more interesting than Helen herself!

Helen Corning's hairstyle and temperament shifted now and then, but her relationship with Nancy didn't: it remained one-dimensional. Helen never earned Nancy's unfailing respect, in part because of her timid nature, in part because of her questionable moral fiber. Helen is the curious type, ever anxious to know the juicy details of Nancy's current cases. But although Helen means well, Nancy doesn't always trust her. This comes through clearly in *The Hidden Staircase* (1930): "Nancy was on the verge of telling Helen about her proposed trip to The Mansion, but she could not bring herself to the point of revealing the secret. Helen's intentions were of the best, but she was a natural born gossip."

The two young women did share one memorable experience in *The Bungalow Mystery* (1930)—a near-drowning at Moon Lake. A fierce summer storm approached, the skies darkened, and their rowboat began to sink. Unfortunately, Helen was better at screaming than swimming, and it was Nancy (with the help of a young rescuer named Laura Pendleton) who saved them from certain death among the turbulent waves.

In the revised text of *The Mystery at Lilac Inn* (1961), Nancy and Helen are involved once again in a boating mishap, but this time Helen is hailed as an excellent swimmer, less skittish and more worldly. Nonetheless, Helen was never a strong enough character to command Nancy's serious attention.

Eventually, Helen Corning disappeared from the stories, but she remains Nancy's first real female chum and an official part of Nancy Drew history.

Bess Marvin and George Fayne

Of all the characters in Nancy's world, George Fayne and Bess Marvin have undergone the most noticeable changes. They were introduced on page one of *The Secret at Shadow Ranch* (1931) as follows: "Nancy Drew, curled up like a contented kitten on the living room davenport, smiled at the earnest entreaties of her friends, Elizabeth Marvin and George Fayne."

That was the first and last time that Bess was ever referred to as "Elizabeth" in the course of the series. In that volume we find out that these close neighbors and former schoolmates of Nancy's are first cousins. They have an Aunt Nell and Uncle Richard Rawley of Chicago who recently acquired a run-down ranch in Arizona. In chapter 1 of *Shadow Ranch*, the cousins implored Nancy to join them for a trip out west to see the ranch—an invitation that led to their first team adventure, and Nancy's first out-of-state case.

As the story progressed, George emerged as the more dominant of the two; she also considerd herself quite homely. When Nancy disputed this, George replied, "Look at this straight hair and my pug nose! And everyone says I'm irresponsible and terribly boyish!"

In the early books George is indifferent to dating, revels in her emotional independence, and seems more comfortable enjoying a cold soda and greasy burger at a truck stop than waltzing at a prom. Her slim figure, tailored clothes, and short-cropped hair accentuate her tomboy image. George is happy and secure in this role, which provides a refreshing change from some of the other, rather mundane and giggle-happy gals of River Heights. (The early George is also level-headed in a crisis, although she frequently screams "yikes!" when faced with a major problem.) She is markedly different

In *The Clue of the Broken Locket* (1934), Nancy, Bess, and George get sidetracked in Nancy's roadster. (Simon & Schuster)

from her cousin Bess, and is an able, honorable accomplice for Nancy Drew.

The early Bess Marvin is distinguished and composed, known for doing the right thing at the right time. In *The Clue of the Tapping Heels* (1939), Bess is described as "a dignified-looking girl who took joy in dressing well." Although she finds fleeting opportunities for flirting and shopping, essentially she is shy and reserved.

Contemporary readers have probably noticed something wrong with this picture. George considered homely and irresponsible? Bess calm and composed?

The George of the 1990s is anything but irresponsible. She is the only one of the trio who routinely holds down a job, whether it's waitressing on weekends or driving a Frosty Freeze ice-cream truck for extra spending money. George is forever practicing for a sports tournament with vigorous discipline or warning everyone about the dangers of irresponsibility. In Nancy Drew Files Case #33, *Danger in Disguise* (1989), George even shows strong civic responsibility by volunteering for a local political campaign. The current George Fayne is five feet eight inches tall, with curly dark hair and dark eyes. The series' current publisher, Simon & Schuster, describes George as "a young Pam Shriver type, good-looking, athletic and courteous." But the new George still says "yikes!"

The new Bess Marvin, on the other hand, is far from composed. She is forever bobbing up and down or "ahhing" or panicking, and she rarely does the right thing at the right time—even though she tries.

This transition started as early as 1946, when Bess is described as a "plump, jolly girl" absolutely obsessed with her looks. By the 1950s, her penchant for shopping, flirting, and personal adornment reached new heights. In more than one instance her vanity led the trio to a new mystery, such as in *The Mystery of the Tolling Bell* (1946), in which she purchased the expensive (and tainted) Mon Coeur line of cosmetics in hopes of making herself more desirable. In fact, she only suffered a hefty financial loss.

Today, Bess still frets about her weight, but she has slimmed down considerably. She is five feet four inches tall with long, straw-blond hair, sparkling blue eyes, and a curvy figure. Her light-hearted flirting has turned into what can only be termed "boy crazy" behavior. She spends a large amount of time falling in and out of love and has a particular preference for movie stars, musicians, and rock music. In Nancy Drew Files Case #36, *Over the Edge* (1989), Bess's new personality is summarized well: "Bess could be in an arctic iceberg and still manage to find a cute guy. She has a two-track mind—boys and food."

The relationship between Bess and George has also shifted through the years. In the original volumes, the pair routinely engaged in heated disagreements. At times, Bess was a simpering victim to her cousin's crude remarks—especially those concerning her weight. After one particular picnic on the prairie, Bess held up her third sandwich and complained that she was getting heavier every day of her life: " 'Fifth [sandwich], you mean,' George corrected her cruelly." The early George (nicknamed "George the Terrible" by some series-book collectors)

The Name Game

George's name has caused controversy in the plots, and among fans, since her debut in the series: "I wonder if the Señora who is headmistress will let George be called George," laughed the housekeeper in *The Mystery of the Brass Bound Trunk* (1940). "She may not approve of a girl who has a boy's name!"

Certainly, a girl with a nickname (or real name) of George does not sit well with many of River Heights' socialites, and her obvious preference for this name confuses friends and foes alike. But the real debate among fans is whether her real name is George or Georgia.

In her debut in *The Secret at Shadow Ranch* (1931), Ms. Fayne stated that she likes her name but gets tired of explaining that it *isn't short for Georgia.* Later in that same volume, she elaborated: "Everyone had given up hope for a boy in our family by the time I came, so I was named George, just plain George, for my grandfather." Another volume says that the Faynes were expecting a boy and therefore named the girl George anyway, but does not mention the grandfather.

On the other hand, in *The Clue in the Old Stagecoach* (1960), we are told George Fayne's real name is Georgia. The blue, tweed-covered volumes of *Stagecoach* call her Georgia on page one, but some copies of the yellow volumes refer to her only as George. The Nancy Drew Files are more consistent on the matter: George's real name is Georgia, and George is a nickname.

was not above calling Bess fat or stupid, or poking fun at her compassionate nature. In *The Whispering Statue* (1937), when the girls found Nancy's soon-to-be pet, Togo, George had a stick ready to strike the pup and merely scoffed at Bess's concern for the terrier's welfare. George's cutting remarks (and her anti-animal attitude) were toned by the 1950s, and the cousins' relationship became much more amicable.

The Six of Us

Like Nancy Drew, both George and Bess date freely but also have steady boyfriends. Many of the most exciting plots in the Nancy Drew Mystery Stories have involved this sixsome teaming up to foil evildoers.

George's special friend is Burt Eddelton (sometimes spelled "Bert"), who is blond, handsome, and full of common sense. Bess prefers the company of Dave Evans, a boy who shares her good humor and preference for pepperoni pizza. Dave has a rangy build, dark hair, and flashing green eyes.

Although their college majors shift from volume to volume, Burt and Dave are definitely great friends of Nancy's beau, Ned Nickerson, and they all play football for Emerson College. The boys often just happen to be traveling to the same places as their girlfriends, which provides bountiful opportunities for the six intelligent, ambitious teens. In *The Hidden Window Mystery* (1956), the girls were in Charlottesville, North Carolina, when they received a message that the boys would be joining them within the next few days for an annual college conference. The timing was perfect, of course, and the mystery at hand was solved in record time.

As the number of cases they solve together adds up, so do the team's abilities for detection. They are outstanding at staking out suspects, pooling their information, and tracking down villains. One of their favorite ploys is to have Nancy lure a criminal down a deserted street and then have Bess or Ned follow him. Burt, Dave, and George position themselves in various hot spots or wait by the phone, and in no time the criminal is trapped like a rat.

The dynamic "six-some"—Nancy and Ned, George and Burt, Bess and Dave—work to-gether in *The Quest of the Missing Map* (1942). (Simon & Schuster)

Let's Do Lunch

Whenever Nancy, George, and Bess drop the boys back at Emerson College and are left to their own devices, they almost always stop for lunch. As a matter of fact, these three spend an inordinate amount of time eating. Not a story (or sometimes not even a chapter) goes by without a nosh of some type.

One of the more memorable Nancy Drew dining experiences occurred in The Mystery of the Tolling Bell (1946). The girls were near the ocean at Whitecap Bay when they stopped at the Wayside Inn, located in the town of Fisher's Grove. As usual, they were famished. They started out with plates of french-fried clams and a huge plate piled high with puffed, breaded shrimp. In addition to the seafood, they ate fresh tomatoes, cabbage salad, potatoes, hot biscuits, and lemonade. For dessert they enjoyed large servings of apple pie. It's not surprising that George said she felt like a puffed shrimp herself after that meal!

The Clue in the Diary (1932), however, set a record for food consumption that has yet to be surpassed. The book contained at least twelve references to eating, as the girls steadily munched their way from River Heights to Stanford and back again. The book started out at a carnival, where Nancy, Bess, and George had consumed hot dogs, peanuts, and sodas. On the way home, they stopped for a relaxing picnic lunch (packed by Hannah Gruen) and plump Bess ate five chicken sandwiches. They hopped back in Nancy's roadster and headed toward River Heights but were delayed by an explosion at the Raybolt estate. Soon their new friend Ned Nickerson treated them to ice-cream sodas at the Mapleton Drug Store. The following day the girls decided to save a child named Honey from certain starvation. They pooled their money and stocked up on food at the grocery store. Of course, this required that they prepare some of it as well, and the entire crew sat down to a feast of steak, vegetables, melons, bread, and ice cream. Before the mystery was solved, they dined heartily at the Maplecroft Inn, and afterward Nancy moved on to Baylor Weston's home for a six-course dinner. The book ended with a gala party at the Drews' house to celebrate another happy ending—with tables fairly groaning with food and drink!

Fortunately, Nancy, Bess, and George rarely suffered from indigestion, and the mysteries carried on.

In all fairness to Carolyn Keene, it should be noted that dining out with Nancy Drew is never a simple event but instead another vehicle for tracking down thieves, eavesdropping on nearby table conversations for clues, or finding lost jewels.

These days, chicken-and-waffle dinners have been replaced with mushroom pizzas at the River Heights Pizza Palace or twelve-foot submarine sandwiches for the group at local gatherings. But the intrigue abounds just the same, and restaurants and picnics are still a source of adventure for the trio—and a source of delight for fans.

The character traits and eating habits of George and her cousin Bess may have changed through the decades, but the girls remain true friends of Nancy Drew. They exhibit perseverance against seemingly insurmountable odds. At times, such as in the 1933 version of *The Sign of the Twisted Candles*, their friendship is tested and almost shattered. In their quest to assist Nancy in searching for truth and justice, the cousins have been knocked down, poisoned, almost drowned, locked up in prison, injured in car crashes, and nearly suffocated in an ice-cream freezer.

Once in a while, as in *The Clue in the Diary* (1932), Bess and George express their doubts about pulling off the seemingly impossible tasks asked of them. But at times like these Nancy simply flashes a winning smile and urges them on: " 'Calm your nerves. Three capable, muscular, brainy girls such as we are shouldn't need any help!' "

And soon, Bess and George are back on the trail of the mystery. You see, it isn't easy being friends with Nancy Drew. But it is irresistible.

A Tangled Web of Love and Romance

Readers of Nancy Drew have often wondered if she and Ned Nickerson would *ever* get married. After all, Ned didn't even propose to her until Nancy Drew Files Case #24, *Till Death Do Us Part*, in 1988—and even then, Nancy is surprised:

> *"You never mentioned wanting to get married before."*
> *"No, but I've been thinking about it. Haven't you?"*
> *Nancy felt her cheeks grow warm.*
> *The truth was, she hadn't.*

Although Ned is rebuffed during this particular exchange, it is clear from the first afternoon Nancy and Ned met back in the 1930s that a special chemistry exists between them, a chemistry fueled by tender moments on the dance floor and dangerous moments fighting off arsonists and kidnappers. Ned is handsome, gallant, and muscular, ready to help Nancy whenever his presence is required. Nancy is intelligent, multi-talented, and refreshingly pretty. Even Nancy's father, Carson Drew, approves wholeheartedly of the match. So why, when Ned finally asked for Nancy's hand in marriage, did she just say no?

Equally important, *will she ever change her mind?*

To answer these questions, one must look back through the myriad romantic adventures in Nancy's life and search for clues to her future with (or without) the young man often referred to by fans as "good old reliable Ned Nickerson."

Models depict Nancy and Ned sharing a tender moment in a Nancy Drew–themed fashion picture for *Mademoiselle* magazine, July 1964. (George Barkentin)

Nancy and Ned's First Meeting

Ned Nickerson first appeared in the seventh book of the series, *The Clue in the Diary,* released in 1932. Nancy was on the scene of her latest caper, snooping about the grounds of the Raybolt estate, which had just exploded. As fire threatened to spread to the area where Nancy's new roadster was parked, she decided she should move it to safer ground.

But when Nancy reached her destination, she stopped in her tracks.

A strange boy was stealing her car!

In typical fashion, Nancy quickly recovered and fearlessly jumped onto the running board of her Model A, not at all pleased with the situation and ready to show her disapproval. " 'Your car, miss?' Ned inquired with a disarming smile."

For once, cool, calm Nancy Drew was indeed disarmed.

"The youth was not more than eighteen or nineteen, Nancy decided, surveying him critically. His hair was dark and slightly curly, his eyes whimsical and friendly."

Ned informed Nancy that he was simply being helpful by removing her shiny blue roadster from the path of the raging flames. Hearing his explanation, Nancy relaxed—a bit. There remained the nagging possibility that, since her car was the most expensive one in the lineup, the young man might have planned on stealing it. But Nancy's suspicions quickly faded as her heart began to flutter under Ned's penetrating gaze. Then, with a friendly nod of farewell, he simply slipped off into the crowd: " 'I don't know what to make of him!' Nancy thought in bewilderment."

Although the mystery at hand was still Nancy's priority in *The Clue in the Diary* (1932), "that Drew girl" did indulge in some rather uncharacteristic behavior throughout the text. When Ned called to offer his assistance on the case, Nancy hung up the phone and "fairly danced back into the bedroom." She sent one slipper flying toward the bed, and the other into the far corner of the room. She attempted to explain her jubilant spirits by telling herself that she was overjoyed at unearthing a possible clue, but her readers knew better. Nancy Drew was smitten.

The tall, handsome boy with the warm blue eyes had captured her heart. She would soon learn to adore his football-star ruggedness, his ambition to graduate from Emerson College and become a successful businessman, his willingness to accept her own independence with such alacrity, *and* his wonderful family. It didn't hurt that he would be spending school breaks at his hometown of Mapleton, just a short distance from River Heights. Even though the revised text of *Diary* (1962) tones down Nancy's emotional response to Ned, readers of either version cannot mistake the change in Nancy from pre-Ned episodes.

Life Before Ned

Prior to their meeting, Nancy dedicated herself to her sleuthing with little interest in romantic meanderings. In the 1959 revised edition of *The Hidden Staircase* we find Nancy helping to plan the wedding of her friend Helen Corning, content in her role as "always a bridesmaid, never a bride." While the other girls are jumping for the bridal bouquet, Nancy is in the powder room.

In *The Hidden Staircase* we also witness a brief incident involving a boy named Dirk Jackson, Nancy's first official date of the series. Nancy and the red-haired former high school tennis champion drove off to pick up another couple and attend a play given by the local theater group, followed by an evening of dancing. That night, Nancy admitted it was fun to be with Dirk and agreed to a future date—after her current mystery was solved. She implied that Dirk was a favorite among her many suitors; however, an early exchange in the book suggests the relationship is doomed:

> "Say, young lady, you'd better go dress for that date of yours," [Carson] winked. "I happen to know that Dirk doesn't like to be kept waiting."
> "Especially by any of my mysteries," Nancy replied.

A boy who dares demean the importance of her career? Exit Dirk Jackson.

References to actual dates with young men are downplayed. For example, in *The Secret of the Old Clock* (1959), Nancy mentions that she has to shop for a new dress to wear to a country club dance, but her escort is never identified.

When *The Bungalow Mystery* was reissued in 1960, readers may have suspected a serious romantic prospect in Nancy's next gentleman caller. While strolling along the tree-lined streets of River Heights, mulling over the theft of some valuable bank securities, Nancy meets Don Cameron. We learn that athletic-looking Don had escorted Nancy to her spring prom, and she readily agrees to be his date at an upcoming barbecue. Before the big day, however, our fickle sleuth changes her plans. Finding herself needed on more pressing business, Nancy decides that Don will have to settle for a "proxy date," and generously offers up the series' latest orphaned victim of crime, fifteen-year-old Laura Pendleton, as her substitute. Nancy thinks this is a perfectly equitable arrangement: "I'll ask Don if he'd mind. If he does—well, that's that."

Predictably, Don doesn't mind at all, considering that Nancy has such important matters to attend to, and he dutifully treats Laura to a night out. Don eventually gets involved in Nancy's case and Nancy is gracious in her appreciation of Don's assistance, yet they part company on noncommittal terms. (Don Cameron reappears in Nancy's life, launching an unsuccessful campaign to win her heart, in Nancy Drew Files Case #27, *Most Likely to Die.*)

Even when Nancy's sleuthing began to take her away from River Heights and into more adventurous settings, she maintained her indifference to deep romantic attachments. In volume #5, *The Secret at Shadow Ranch* (1931), Bess Marvin dreamily discussed the attractive, rugged-looking boys they might encounter upon reaching her aunt's ranch in Arizona, to which Nancy simply smiled and replied, "I'll leave the cowboys to you since I don't have a flair for the romantic."

The Rules of the Mating Game

This type of take-'em-or-leave-'em attitude dominated the series until Ned was introduced as a major character. No prior suitor had ever made Nancy "blush to her fingertips" like her fraternity boy with the disarming grin. This is not to imply that Ned changed Nancy's mind about the role of romance in her life. In fact, the final chapter of *The Clue in the Diary* (revised text, 1962) drives home Nancy's priorities:

> *"Say," said Ned, "I have a notion to start a diary of my own!"*
> *"Why don't you?" Nancy asked lightly. She became conscious that*

Ned's eyes were looking straight at her.

"I will if I can fill most of the pages with entries of dates with you."

Nancy evaded the question. "I enjoyed your help in solving the Swenson mystery. Maybe we'll soon find another one we can work on together."

And so the pattern was set.

Ned occasionally expressed interest in a more permanent arrangement, but Nancy always managed to avoid further discussion of the topic.

Ned is present in well over half the Nancy Drew Mystery Stories. Yet neither he nor any other man except her father has ever overshadowed her inherent curiosity, her penchant for adventure, or her desire to leave her mark on society. Nancy Drew was the first teen heroine to operate as a full-time detective, and she was quick to cancel a party or date if the opportunity for an engagement with a suspicious character arose. This may have proved inconvenient to her suitors and friends, but Nancy was too focused to let that get in the way of her goals.

In *Seventeen* magazine (May 1984), Joanne Furtak phrased it well when she said, "Nancy enjoyed male company but knew there were more important things in life. After her first date with handsome Ned Nickerson, Nancy went to bed dreaming of clues, not kisses. She was a feminist's dream before the dream became fashionable, a Gloria Steinem without an air of defiance."

In order to maintain this image, Ned Nickerson was kept safely in Nancy's shadow. When he did wander into the path of Nancy's work, he was there to protect or assist her so she could get on with her crime-solving.

Ned's baritone voice, with its ring of authority, often proves helpful in bringing chaos into order. In *The Whispering Statue* (1937), a large, unruly crowd had gathered about the lake where Nancy and her friends were searching for a valuable pocketbook. Nancy quickly asked Ned to move the people away before someone fell into the lake. He did so winningly. Most advantageous of all was the way Ned took directions from Nancy without making a fuss: "Ned did not annoy the girls with any useless questions."

Yes, Ned was just what a girl like Nancy needed!

Ned Nickerson looks on as Nancy finds a clue in The Elusive Heiress (1982). (Simon & Schuster)

Love Comes of Age

The majority of Nancy and Ned's early interludes involve fact-finding missions, double dates, and large group gatherings (often at restaurants), with an occasional moonlight stroll or quiet swim slipping past the publisher's censor. In the volumes produced during the mid-1930s and into the '40s, Ned operated primarily as a plot-resolution device. But he was also perpetually urging Nancy to relax, to have some fun, and to partake in "normal" activities like sports events, hayrides, and tea dances. To insure that she did, Ned often took matters into his own hands.

In *The Mystery of the Brass Bound Trunk* (1940) Ned organized a gala barbecue party in Nancy's honor before she set off for South America, and in *The Clue of the Tapping Heels* (1939) he invited Nancy for a steamer ride on the Muskoka River, where his college club had chartered the Goodtime Cruise Line. There they shared a candlelit dinner, exchanged pleasantries, and delighted in orchestral music. Ned is ever full of touching, romantic ways to win his lady's heart, and once in a while she even softened—until the next needy orphan, sinister villain, or threatening note caught her sparkling blue eyes.

As the series progressed, Ned underwent his own metamorphosis. He was first introduced as captain of Emerson's football team but later emerged as a star baseball and basketball player. His career goals also vacillated with his ambition. In *Nancy Drew Files Case #35, Bad Medicine* (1989), Ned is enrolled in a week-long seminar at Westmoor University Medical School in River Heights, where he is studying hospital administration. *The Mystery of the Fire Dragon* (1961) opens with Nancy reading a letter from Ned, who "likes being a college exchange student in Hong Kong and has learned to speak some Cantonese." Nancy adds later that Ned's goal is to go into the United States Intelligence Service. In other books, Ned is described as a young man destined for law, for business administration, even for athletic coaching.

In the late 1940s, readers and journalists started grumbling about Ned: Ned isn't strong enough for her ... he is too bland . . . he never complains . . . he is just there to fix her car or punch an especially sinister villain. Although these interpretations had some merit, Ned's personality flaws weren't as bad as the critics made them out to be. First of all, Ned didn't appear in every book, so Nancy often had to drive her own car, karate-kick her way out of locked buildings, or repair a flat tire alone.

Second, Ned wasn't always Mr. Nice Guy. The early Ned was certainly easygoing and tolerant with his famous girlfriend but could also be petulant, moody, even aggressive at times, especially toward his competition. In the 1936 edition of *The Mystery of the Ivory Charm*, Ned whisked Nancy off to the Omega fraternity house at Emerson College for a formal party, no doubt looking forward to a few intimate moments on the dance floor. Ned's fraternity brothers were so taken with Nancy, however, that Ned barely saw her all evening. When Ned could endure it no longer, he cut in on the East Indian boy who then had Nancy's attention: " 'Nancy and I have this dance,' Ned told the Hindu. 'It's time for you to scram . . . that's an English slang word meaning go—leave—depart. Unless you do I'll be tempted to challenge you to a duel at sunrise!' "

Ned got his dance.

The syndicate did eventually give in to requests from the public and began to alter Ned's character. He was gradually awarded more responsibility. He demonstrated his intelligence with helpful bits of knowledge he passed along to Nancy when she was stumped on a case (like Carson Drew, he's a whiz at rock formations), and most important, his heartfelt adoration for Nancy developed a foundation of respect to sustain it. He stopped putting Nancy on a pedestal or uttering worshipful praises such as the one in *Nancy's Mysterious Letter* (1932): "If you want me to dress in feathers and war paint and play the Scotch bag-pipes up and down Main Street, I'll do it without asking you why!" Gems like these were deleted from the revised texts.

Ned and Nancy's relationship continued to undergo subtle shifts, in keeping with societal preferences, throughout the late 1960s and well into the '70s. But while thousands of young people were exploring free love, rock and roll, and mind-altering experiences, Nancy and her "special friend" were still innocently sharing double-dip sundaes, tracking art thieves in River Heights, or exposing crocodile poachers in Florida. Ned remained true-blue, even as life with Nancy became increasingly risky. In *Mystery of the Glowing Eye* (1974) Ned is kidnapped, in *The Ghost of Blackwood Hall* (1967) he is plunged into quicksand, in *The Hidden Window Mystery* (1956) he is threatened by a wild dog, and in *The Secret of the Golden Pavilion* (1959) he and Nancy are almost consumed by killer sharks!

When the couple was brought to television in the 1977 network series "Hardy Boys/Nancy Drew Mysteries," Nancy and Ned's lives reached new levels of excitement in living color, but their wholesome value system remained intact. Nancy's chastity and her steady relationship with Ned were always mandatory when Grosset & Dunlap and Harriet S. Adams plotted her fate. Nancy never moved past the hand-holding stage, with the exception of a platonic kiss or a "tender rush" of feeling.

But that was destined to change.

When Simon & Schuster began publishing Drew titles in paperback format, Nancy Drew took on a new wardrobe and more liberal attitudes. This was a gradual process that did not really alter the basic structure of the texts until 1985, after Simon & Schuster had purchased the Stratemeyer Syndicate outright. At that time the editors undertook a major overhaul of Nancy's image.

In an interview with the author, series ghostwriter Jim Lawrence recalled that time in Nancy Drew's history: "I had been ghostwriting for the syndicate for over twenty years and had written or revised a lot of titles for them in The Hardy Boys, Chris Cool, and Tom Swift, Jr. series, all of which had been originally released by Grosset & Dunlap. Late in 1984, the editor in charge of the Nancy Drew series at Simon & Schuster called me and asked if I'd write a few titles. She told me to work on an updated profile of Nancy . . . to make her more contemporary. I agreed, and then I asked the big questions: Can Nancy date boys other than Ned Nickerson? Can she kiss them? 'Yes,' she said."

Jim went to work on *The Bluebeard Room*, which was released in 1985 as #77 in the series. A great number of parents that year (many of whom had been Drew fans themselves in younger days) did a double take when they peeked into this edition of Nancy Drew and saw lines like these:

> *"You sure know how to keep a date!" Nancy laughed, and kissed Alan on the cheek.*
> *"Hey, don't I rate one?" Lance complained, so she kissed him too.*

In *The Bluebeard Room*, Nancy has two young men anxious for her charms: Alan Trevor, a reporter, and Lance Warrick, superstar singer in a band called the Crowned Heads. Most of the book takes place in England, complete with the haunting gothic overtones that characterize so many Drew titles. But this time an adult chaperon (along with Bess, George, and Ned) is conspicuously missing, and Nancy leaves River Heights unencumbered to solve the sinister secret of the Cornwall cliffs. Along the way, her alleged affair with the punk rocker makes tabloid headlines and she is even caught with a package of cocaine in her pocketbook (which she duly passes along to the authorities). This adventure shows a more risqué side of Nancy, a side that is further developed with the next volume in the series.

In *The Phantom of Venice* (1985), Nancy sets out for Venice to help her father solve a bizarre kidnapping. This mystery challenges Nancy's libido as much as her sleuthing abilities. Her first thought as she takes off in the plane from Kennedy Airport is "Am I or am I not in love with Ned Nickerson?" This line alone is an eye-catcher for readers, but things become even more complicated when Nancy arrives at her destination and confronts evildoer Gianni Spinelli:

> There was a certain glitter in his luminous dark eyes, and a feline grace to his rippling muscular movements which seemed to hint that he could be as cruel and heartless as he was handsome. . . . [He had] an arrogantly sensual glance—a smiling macho challenge, loaded with frank and open desire.

This is decidedly spicy for a Nancy Drew mystery and a sure-fire challenge for Nancy's calm demeanor. Fortunately, she does not give in to Gianni's charms but instead brings him to justice. She does, however, fall for a gentleman named Don Madison who helps her on a stakeout one night. One thing leads to another, until:

> Don was holding her tight now, and her arms were around his neck and their lips were meeting in a kiss that was warm and loving and exciting and oh, so tender! It seemed to Nancy that she'd never, ever felt about anyone the way she felt about Don Madison at that moment.

During this particular case, it seems as if Ned Nickerson is about to become history. The book ends on a "to be continued" note, an unforgettable romantic cliff-hanger. Later volumes of the series show Nancy and Ned back together, but readers continue to wonder whether young Don Madison will be back.

Nancy and Ned: The Future

The Ned Nickerson of today is more clearly defined. The current Nancy Drew mysteries describe him as six foot two, with a square jawline and classic good looks. He is an honor student at Emerson College and reigning captain of the football team. His aspirations are managerial. The couple have their favorite spots, including the Pizza Palace and the dance floor at the River Heights Café. These days, they snuggle in front of cozy fires at ski resorts and Nancy becomes "more breathless" after their goodnight kisses. But most important, Ned is still available for international adventures with his main gal, Nancy Drew. His quick reflexes and equally quick-thinking mind work in perfect harmony with hers.

Although their relationship is not without problems, Ned and Nancy will most likely always return to each other's arms. In both the Nancy Drew Mystery Stories and the Nancy Drew Files, this duo has survived a considerable amount of growing pains. They have both enjoyed the company of other mates; they have both been unjustly rude to each other; and they have both wondered, Is this really the person for me?

In spite of these low points, Ned and Nancy are quite compatible and most fans are comfortable with their relationship. In *The Bluebeard Room* (1985) we learn that "Nancy had had one or two romantic encounters which struck sparks, but Ned remained always in the back of her mind as someone safe and rocklike and comforting—someone she could always count on and turn to, no matter how the shifting winds of fancy might blow."

Ned enjoys the challenge of dating America's favorite teen sleuth—even if he is continually putting his life in danger by doing so. In short, Nancy and Ned make a good team, and most fans see no reason for that to change. Even with the "raciness" that has slipped into the recent texts, the partnership remains decidedly innocent and beyond reproach. Nancy is still determinedly in control of her heartstrings and has avoided the topic of love for more than fifty years.

Not until the Nancy Drew Files Case #15, *Trial By Fire* (1987), do Nancy and Ned break series precedent and declare their true feelings for each other. After a kiss, Ned nuzzles Nancy's ear and says the magic words:

> "I love you, Nancy Drew."
> Nancy felt so content that she was ready to purr. "And I love you too, Ned Nickerson," she said. "Probably always will."

Declarations of love aside, fans can be sure that Nancy's relationship with Ned, or with any other boy, will *never* reach the point of marriage. The reason we are given is that Nancy wants her career firmly established before she even considers the idea of a permanent relationship, and Ned, regardless of his weak moments, both respects and agrees with this philosophy. But the primary reason that Ned and Nancy will never truly join is one of pure economics. As previous series proved, when an independent heroine like Nancy Drew decides to tie the knot, the readership drops—drastically.

In the golden days of the Stratemeyer Syndicate, the series character Ruth Fielding exemplified the rags-to-riches saga. Ruth was introduced in 1913 as a poor orphan, and by the thirtieth volume in the series, in 1934, she had become a successful movie producer and was awarded the title of Duchess of Sharlot. The books had an enormous audience and Ruth, like Nancy Drew, was a top-notch sleuth and an extremely liberated heroine. But unlike Nancy, Ruth decided to get married. Juggling career, marriage, and children soon proved too much of a burden—for the character, the author, and the readership. The series was discontinued, and by then Nancy Drew was the reigning queen of girls' series.

After that, the syndicate made it an ironclad rule never to marry off its lead characters. Meanwhile, another popular girls' heroine shared a similar fate with Ruth Fielding. Judy Bolton, a famous sleuth created by Margaret Sutton, flourished from 1932 to 1967. Her series boasted a loyal, constant readership . . . until Judy married and reality intruded. The result? A drop in sales.

Young girls reading these books were unwilling to trade mystery, suspense, and danger for marital bliss and career ambivalence. What the readers wanted most of all was the freedom their heroines enjoyed—uncluttered by domestic realities.

The closest Nancy ever came to thinking about tying the knot was in Nancy Drew Files Case #35, *Bad Medicine* (1985). After watching a couple she knows eagerly discuss marriage plans (*after* their careers are set), Nancy dreamily reflects that someday she'd like to make such plans too. Ned and Nancy share a tender moment . . . but it is short-lived. Soon she is back in her Mustang, checking to make sure her flashlight and picklock are ready for action . . . and Ned is safely reinstated at Emerson.

Shortly before her death, Harriet S. Adams gave an interview to *Redbook* magazine in honor of Nancy Drew's fifty-year anniversary in the publishing world. Discussing Nancy "then and now," Mrs. Adams said, "Fifty years ago Nancy Drew was considered independent. Today she is liberated. Lately she's taken up kissing. But Nancy will never get married because Ned Nickerson can't corner her long enough to ask her and I don't plan to give him the opportunity."

Nancy Drew's new publishers, Simon & Schuster, have held to the Stratemeyers' policy of keeping Nancy single, and there is every indication that they will continue to do so. Like Nancy herself, her romance will never age.

Nancy Drew on Stage and Screen

The Nancy Drew Movies and Television Series

Bonita Granville, continuing her Nancy Drew characterization, is a demon reporter to obliterate the memory of Richard Harding Davis, as well as a sleuth to send J. Edgar Hoover back to playing cops and robbers with the neighborhood urchins. Nothing like the story could ever happen on land or sea, but the kids will lap it up.
—*Variety* magazine review of *Nancy Drew: Reporter*, 1938

The Silver Screen

The reviewers were right! The four Nancy Drew movies, produced by Warner Brothers, played the "B" spot of double-feature matinees across the United States in 1938 and 1939. *Variety* coined them "comic-strip thrillers" and "bread 'n' butter pictures for the moppets," hailing them for their lickety-split action scenes and the stars' comedic antics. Sure, the plots were implausible, the fare too light for adults, the song-and-dance scenes hokey, but overall they were pure fun. As one reviewer put it, they were "guaranteed to keep the juve element hopping or your money back by return post."

Contemporary Nancy Drew fans are often shocked to learn there was a string of Nancy Drew "comedramas." For a long time, even collectors of Nancy Drew movie memorabilia were unaware of the string of events that led to the productions. But in recent years actor Frankie Thomas, who portrayed Ted (not Ned) Nickerson on screen, was interviewed for several magazines and radio shows about his work on the Drew movies; he shed light on some interesting behind-the-scenes tidbits.

How it all began is Hollywood folklore worthy of more than a footnote in Nancy Drew's history. The head of Warner

Brothers' B productions in the late 1930s was Bryan Foy—one of the original "seven little Foys" of vaudeville fame. His beloved daughter, Bonnie, wanted one thing for Christmas: a complete set of Nancy Drews, which at that time included fourteen volumes. Bryan sent one of his legmen to the Broadway Hollywood to find the books, but they were sold out everywhere. In a 1990 interview on KCRW-FM (Santa Monica, California), Frankie Thomas recalled that Bryan responded to the problem gleefully: "Well, if they're that popular, let's look into it!"

The film rights were secured, contract actors chosen for the leads, the preview publicity "leaked" in record time. The only thing that lagged were the scripts. Warner went through at least three writers before deciding, in typical Hollywood fashion, to emphasize the "boy-girl" angle—not the serious, independent qualities of Nancy Drew and her girlfriends. The studio wanted its own innocuous male/female counterparts to the popular Andy Hardy movies starring Mickey Rooney and Judy Garland. Even though Frankie Thomas, (unlike Rooney) was taller than his lovely co-star, Bonita Granville, the team was lauded as a good match, and the movies enjoyed critical success. The studio even managed to keep a sliver of the original Nancy Drew plots intact—although Bess Marvin and George Fayne were deleted from the movies as too ho-hum, and housekeeper Hannah Gruen was replaced by the more animated (and silly) Effie.

> **There were four Nancy Drew films:**
> Nancy Drew: Detective (December 1938)
> Nancy Drew: Reporter (March 1939)
> Nancy Drew: Trouble Shooter (September 1939)
> Nancy Drew and the Hidden Staircase (November 1939)

As Frankie Thomas told *Yellowback Library* interviewer Gregory Jackson, Jr., during the eighteen-month period he and Granville were filming the episodes they had only eight days off, and six of those were because Ms. Granville developed intestinal flu. Ned Nickerson's name was changed to Ted because "Ned" was considered old-fashioned.

Thomas recalled one memorable scene in which Carson Drew carries Nancy off to her room singing "Good Night Ladies" (when she really wanted to stay up and talk about the

Frankie Thomas and Bonita Granville play "Ted" and Nancy in this 1938 publicity photo for *Nancy Drew: Reporter.*

case) was completely improvised by veteran actor John Litel during rehearsal. The director loved it and the scene survived the final cut.

The movies did not depict the true Nancy Drew, of course, but that was not their purpose. They were designed as light entertainment, not to rival *Gone with the Wind.* The mystery elements were used merely to spice up the plot and to translate the popularity of Nancy Drew, fictional heroine, into profits for Nancy Drew, screen princess.

Like the real sleuth, Granville's Nancy was energetic, tenacious, and consumed with curiosity. One reviewer compared her to an "alert, fearless Scottie pup . . . always poking her nose into hornet's nests . . . always thwarting the devious plans of the rogues she uncovers." Yet unlike Carolyn Keene's Nancy, Granville blatantly used her feminine wiles (and enticing bribes) to persuade Ted Nickerson to perform her dirty work, which at one point landed timid, small-framed Ted in a boxing ring with a large professional thug.

Frankie Thomas played straight man to Bonita's Nancy with great skill. They continued as a team for many other movies, including *Angels Wash Their Faces*, with Ronald Reagan. Thomas eventually made the transition from big screen to television in the 1950s, impressing boys across America as spaceman Tom Corbett.

Under the creative direction of William Clemens, the supporting actors were encouraged to add a personal touch to their characters. This usually surfaced in the form of slapstick. To fill the void of Nancy's missing chums, writer Kenneth Gamet created a bratty kid brother and sister for Ted. Their comic antics fill in the lean plots and drive Nancy Drew to distraction. The local police are on hand, as Irish as all River Heights' men in blue, but the books' Chief McGinnis is replaced by Inspector Milligan in *Nancy Drew: Detective* and by Captain Tweedy in *Nancy Drew and the Hidden Staircase*, both skittishly played by Frank Orth. During one petulant moment in *Hidden Staircase*, Bonita Granville refers to him as a "conceited tweet-tweet"—a show of disrespect the real Nancy wouldn't dream of!

In the "who's who" trivia department, we find that in the fourth film, *Nancy Drew and the Hidden Staircase*, young "De Wolf" Hopper portrayed one of the reporters. Twenty years later he would become cult hero private eye Paul Drake in the "Perry Mason" television series under his real name, William Hopper. The offspring of Hollywood gossip columnist Hedda Hopper, he originally used his middle name, De Wolf, to avoid being recognized as Hedda's son.

All four Nancy Drew movies had simple plots. In *Nancy Drew: Reporter*, for example, high schooler Nancy wins the River Heights *Chronicle*'s circulation-building contest. Her prize is a stint as a reporter. Miss Drew finds her assignment from the managing editor much too mundane: she scoffs at the thought of covering a local society function. Instead, she steals another reporter's story involving a nice, juicy murder. That way, Nancy can track down the weapon (poison), sneak into abandoned houses, and clear the name of the beautiful woman accused of cold-hearted murder.

In between chase scenes, the cast would break for a song. One of the highlights of *Nancy Drew: Reporter* is the scene in which Nancy, Ted, and Ted's young sidekicks Mary and Dickie go into a Chinese restaurant to track down a crook. After they eat, they realize they haven't enough money to pay the bill. They are saved from washing dishes when the owner agrees to let them perform in lieu of the cash. Naturally, the restaurant has a large stage and full orchestra on site in the middle of the day. Actress Mary Lee belts out a string of nursery rhymes in a voice worthy of Judy Garland and Nancy's chorus of "Little Bo Peep" goes well with the crowd. It's total thirties camp, but all part of the fun.

The films captured the Drew's River Heights home in grand

Nancy Drew: Detective

Warner Bros. production and release. Features Bonita Granville, John Litel, James Stephenson, Frankie Thomas. Directed by William Clemens. Original screenplay by Kenneth Gamet; based on story by Carolyn Keene; camera, L. William O'Connell; dialog director, John Langan; editor, Frank Magce. At Fox, Brooklyn, week Dec. 1, '38; dual bill. Running time, 67 mins.

Nancy Drew	Bonita Granville
Carson Drew	John Litel
Challon	James Stephenson
Ted Nickerson	Frankie Thomas
Inspector Milligan	Frank Orth
Effie Schneider	Renie Riano
Mary Eldridge	Helena Phillips Evans
Hollister	Charles Trowbridge
Keifer	Dick Purcell
Adam Thorne	Ed Keane
Dr. Spires	Brandon Tynan
Miss Van Deering	Vera Lewis
Miss Tyson	Moe Busch
Spud Murphy	Tommy Rupp
Mrs. Spires	Lottie Williams

style and with impressive accuracy. From the sunny breakfast room to the double garage, from Nancy's canopy bed to Carson's rose garden, the sets turned the fantasy of fiction into big-screen reality. Nancy's snappy roadster, in which she raced about town well beyond the speed limit and crashed a number of times, was equally true to form. The villains were appropriately seedy, challenging Nancy in formidable battles. And in the end, Nancy always won the war. The evildoers were toted to police headquarters to pay their dues to society and everyone forgave the girl sleuth for speeding, stealing, and bribing her way to victory.

Throughout the hullabaloo, the Stratemeyer Syndicate was unusually silent. They reportedly did not even send representatives to the film sites. The only mass-market connection between the Nancy Drew books and the movies occurred in 1938. One print run of *Password to Larkspur Lane* was released by Grosset & Dunlap with a special paper wrapper advertising the film. It read: "This is the book from which the Warner Bros. Photoplay—Nancy Drew: Detective was made."

Harriet S. Adams reportedly was not pleased with the liberties taken with the stories of Carolyn Keene. It would be many years before the syndicate approved another adaptation of Nancy Drew.

In the meantime, the four Nancy Drew movies are available through video rental stores and for sale through specialty dealers. They are also broadcast twice a year or so on late-night television.

And here is an unsolved mystery for movie buffs: Frankie Thomas said that he had the distinct impression he and Bonita Granville did more than four Nancy Drew movies. He was uncertain what became of them. Could there be a "lost" film reel among the archives of Warner Brothers Pictures, Inc.?

Only time will tell.

This paper wrapper appeared on one printing of *The Password to Larkspur Lane* in 1938 to advertise the recently released movie *Nancy Drew: Detective*.

Nancy's Television Debut

It is seven o'clock Sunday night, February 6, 1977. Millions of girls are tuned in to ABC for the premier of "The Nancy Drew Mysteries." Would Pamela Sue Martin, in the starring role, fulfill their fantasies of America's favorite teen sleuth? One week before, heart throbs Shaun Cassidy and Parker Stevenson had certainly pleased viewers in the roles of Joe and Frank Hardy, Nancy Drew's male counterparts. Would Pamela Sue gain equal acclaim? The acting credits roll by . . . Nancy Drew covers from the past two decades flash onto the screen . . . the musical score is appropriately upbeat and intriguing . . .

What followed were sixty minutes of action-based drama with the 1970s version of Nancy Drew solving her first television mystery. The show premiered in conjunction with the new Nancy Drew Mystery Stories volume #54, *Strange Message in the Parchment*. The show did well in the ratings: that week it outranked other detective series like "Kojak," "Barnaby Jones," "Starsky & Hutch," and even "Police Woman."

Yet in the end, the program received mixed reviews. It would take another six months before it reached its peak of

Pamela Sue Martin played Nancy Drew and William Schallert played Carson in "The Nancy Drew Mysteries" TV series. (Universal City Studios/MCA)

popularity. It would also undergo marked changes in the cast, format, even the length of George Fayne's hair, before the final episode aired on January 1, 1978. Even though the "Hardy Boys/Nancy Drew Mysteries" was moderately successful—especially in launching the careers of its stars and inspiring a flurry of spin-off products destined to become Nancy Drew collectibles—the series was not the unparalleled success the network expected. It is difficult to transpose any fictional heroine to the screen, and with Nancy Drew one can safely triple that challenge. Her readers have such lofty expectations for the girl who can do "just about anything" that meeting them is almost impossible. Still, most of the episodes were executed with taste and careful attention to detail, and the cast and crew deserve praise for developing high-quality Sunday night entertainment suitable for the entire family.

The road to that first episode was a long and hard one for the ambitious, talented pair who conceived the idea. The producers for the series were Joyce Brotman and Arlene Sidaris. Both women had worked their way up the administrative ranks of the movie and television industries, eventually meeting in November 1974. At that time, each was anxious for a career change, and they decided to take a shot at becoming producers.

They both felt the Nancy Drew and Hardy Boys books were television naturals, and on February 1, 1975, they optioned the rights from the Stratemeyer Syndicate for The Hardy Boys,

---

The Cast of "The Nancy Drew Mysteries"

Aired on ABC, Sunday nights, 7 to 8 P.M.
February 6, 1977–January 1, 1978

Nancy Drew: Pamela Sue Martin
and Janet Louise Johnson (last four episodes)
Carson Drew: William Schallert
Ned Nickerson: George O'Hanlon, Jr.
George Fayne: Jean Rasey, then Susan Buckner
Bess Marvin: Ruth Cox

which gave them permission to develop the popular book characters into a series, then sell it to a studio or network. In due time they also secured the option on Nancy Drew.

In *Nancy Drew and the Hardy Boys* (Scholastic Books, 1977), Joyce Brotman said that the syndicate kept a close eye on their progress: "They sold us the option because our whole idea was to maintain the wholesomeness of the characters, not to hold them up to ridicule or make hippies out of them." She said Harriet S. Adams and her partner, Nancy Axelrod, required script approval and were active participants in the development process.

Joyce and Arlene prepared an elaborate presentation package and sold the project to Universal Studios. The search was on for talented actors to fill the leading roles. The scripts were written in record time; the writers and technical staff worked eighteen hours a day. The program was slotted as a winter replacement series beginning on January 31, 1977. Behind the scenes, the crew had less than a month to get the first Hardy Boys and Nancy Drew episodes completely finished.

Glen Larson, the executive producer, wrote the scripts and the theme music for the first shows. The episodes were not based on particular Nancy Drew books, but did use key components (often, the names of book characters) as a foundation for new story lines. In "The Secret of the Whispering Walls" an intruder breaks into the Drew home and two elderly spinsters are plunged into panic when ghosts start haunting their estate.

The episode was wonderfully reminiscent of the second Nancy Drew volume, *The Hidden Staircase*, down to the subplot of Nancy finding a secret tunnel dating back to the Revolutionary War times. River Heights' local police chief was changed to a sheriff, but he retained the strong Irish accent he had in the books and Nancy Drew movies.

Unlike the original stories, the new television series portrayed Nancy Drew not as a blonde but as a brunette, and she was not simply an amateur detective. She was a part-time private investigator with serious intentions to make a successful career out of her sleuthing abilities. In "The Mystery at Pirate's Cove," Nancy Drew's father complains to Ned Nickerson: "The day she started part-time investigative work for me was the beginning of my gray hairs." But he was proud of his daughter's accomplishments, just as he was in the books.

TV's Nancy had a medium blue sedan and was the most popular girl in town. In her leading role, Pamela Sue Martin was always flanked by special guest stars. In "The Mystery of the Solid Gold Kicker," handsome Mark Harmon portrayed a football hero framed for murder, and actor Joe Penny made his television debut in one of the premier episodes. (He would go on to become a star in his own right in the "Jake and the Fat Man" series years later.) Actors like Lorne Greene and Paul Williams helped add appeal to both the Hardy Boys and Nancy Drew episodes.

Two newcomers were cast as George Fayne and Ned Nickerson. Actors Jean Rasey and George O'Hanlon, Jr., took on the roles, with ambivalent viewer response. Mail poured in from the very beginning, demanding why "boyish George Fayne" had long brown hair instead of a short-cropped style— and where was Bess Marvin? Jean Rasey soon cut her hair to please fans, and the character of Bess was added to the cast in the second season. Ned also received mixed reviews. Actor George O'Hanlon, Jr., was not the tall, dark, and handsome type, but instead was rather timid and wore glasses! In "The Mystery at Pirate's Cove" the show opens at a dance, with Nancy in the arms of another good-looking local. On the sidelines, George Fayne urges Ned to admit his true feelings for Nancy: wouldn't he like to be the one to take Nancy on a midnight stroll? Ned refuses, insisting that he simply works for Nancy's father as a law clerk and his attraction for Nancy Drew is purely professional admiration and "friendship." Still, Ned is obviously pleased when Nancy casts a winning smile his way.

Shortly after its debut, the series underwent major changes in format, which added to its problems. At first, the Hardy Boys and Nancy Drew shows aired on alternating Sundays. In the fall of 1977, all three sleuths appeared together in a few episodes. In February 1978, the two programs were combined into one, with the three leads sharing the limelight. Unhappy with this arrangement, Pamela Sue Martin left the show, and eighteen-year-old Janet Louise Johnson finished out the last four episodes.

During the filming of the final episodes of the television show, Pamela Sue Martin triggered a flurry of public scorn when she decided to pose for *Playboy* magazine. She appeared on the cover of the July 1978 issue, wearing a seductively draped trench coat and playing her magnifying glass on a "clue" of a cutout bunny. After serving as a role model for countless teenagers, Ms. Martin was featured in a special lingerie pictorial that wasn't especially racy, but nevertheless raised eyebrows across the country. In that article, Pamela Sue said one person charged her with "dispelling all my illusions about Nancy Drew," to which Martin replied: "What the hell do you think? You think I am Nancy Drew? How naive can you get?" This was a far cry from a prior interview in *Nancy Drew and the Hardy Boys* during her reign as Nancy, when she said she absolutely loved the show and couldn't imagine ever getting tired of the role. "I like the character too much," she chimed. "Nancy Drew is out of sight!"

Pamela Sue Martin told *Playboy* that her main reason for leaving the television show was that her diminished role, a result of the merger of Nancy Drew with the Hardy Boys into one bigger-than-life detective team, was not demanding enough. She also wanted to present another side of herself, an image that was a departure from being "as bland as a glass of milk." (She later achieved her goal by portraying vixen Fallon Carrington on ABC's "Dynasty.") And she was probably right that few Nancy Drew television fans bought that particular issue of *Playboy*.

The Nancy Drew character was dropped from the television script altogether in the fall of 1978. At that time, the title, "Hardy Boys/Nancy Drew Mysteries," was shortened to "The Hardy Boys Mysteries," and teen idols Parker Stevenson and Shaun Cassidy carried on without her until August 1979.

That was the last time Nancy Drew made it to network television.

A decade later, a Canadian production company started filming another Nancy Drew television series starring Margot Kidder (of *Superman* movie fame), but when Ms. Kidder was seriously injured in the course of the shooting, the project was canned. Ms. Kidder's own daughter was to star as Nancy Drew, and Margot Kidder was slotted as Nancy's mother, Mrs. Drew!

Since all Drew fans know that Nancy's mother died mysteriously when Nancy was a child, we can only assume that the production company planned to revive her.

As the saying goes, that's show biz.

Nancy Drew on Stage

The daring exploits and intriguing personality of Nancy Drew, fictional detective, have inspired writers, choreographers, artists, and composers across America to bring her to life on the stage. With few exceptions, the audiences who filled the theaters for these productions were delighted with the results.

There is no accurate count of the number of times Nancy Drew Mystery Stories have been adapted, or satirized, for the stage. Not all presentations were widely publicized, and others never even made it to show time. The performances highlighted in this chapter all premiered after 1979. Each reflected the interpretations of its creators and performers, and no two were alike.

Trixie True, Teen Detective The Musical

This off Broadway musical opened in December 1980 at Lucille Lortel's Theater deLys in Manhattan, and it closed shortly thereafter.

Trixie True was a parody of girls' series-book characters, especially Nancy Drew. The script and lyrics were written by Kelly Hamilton, with choreography by Arthur Faria. The production was advertised as "a wild and funny musical . . . an outrageous spoof. A must see." Reviewers from the New York Daily News and other newspapers and magazines did not agree, however, and panned it miserably. (In all fairness it must be acknowledged that one critic for New York magazine was not exactly Nancy's biggest fan. Part of the review read: "You cannot really spoof something that is as trivial, ridiculous and passé as Nancy Drew is to begin with.")

Almost everyone liked the set, however. Designed by Michael J. Hotopp and Paul DePass, it featured a Manhattan office that literally changed before the audience's eyes. *New York Times* critic Frank Rich explained how "with the greatest of ease, its walls fly away to reveal other settings as a pink-on-pink bathroom, a small-town soda shop, a radio station and even a submerged submarine."

The plot of *Trixie True* revolved around a crazed aspiring mystery novelist named Joe who was forced to ghostwrite Trixie books to survive. He decided to gain notoriety by killing off Trixie in her latest episode, *The Secret of the Tapping Shoes*, and although he did not succeed with his dastardly plan he was nonetheless plunged into a world of international spies, sex-crazed women, and exploding shoes. The musical number featured throughout the show was "This Is Indeed My Lucky Day."

Trixie True was staged as a "show within a show," with the plot revolving around Joe's plan for Trixie's demise intertwined with the actual plight of Trixie when she is brought to life from out of a book's pages. Unusual characters included a transvestite German spy and a boyfriend named Dick Dickerson vying for laughs.

There were two main criticisms of *Trixie True*. Walter Kerr pointed out in the *New York Times* that it was unclear what exactly was being parodied: "Was [the author, Hamilton] going to make happy hash of the girl detective theme . . . on his heroine

---

The Cast of Trixie True, Teen Detective

Joe	Gene Lindsay
Al and Wilhelm	Jay Lowman
Miss Snood and Mme. Olga	Marilyn Sokol
Trixie True	Kathy Adrini
Dick Dickerson	Keith Rice
Laverne	Alison Bevan
Maxine	Mariana Allen
Bobby	Keith Caldwell

as All-American Overachiever . . . or the hard-working hack who was writing stories?" Or was it something else?

The second problem was that the musical was not played as a perfectly straight satire. Frank Rich made the distinction between a forced parody like Trixie True and a play like Annie that is indeed played straight, right until the end, with humor deriving naturally from the characters' actions and reactions. In the end, Annie audiences felt good about themselves and the topic of the play—they did not feel embarrassed by it.

Clearly, many members of Trixie True's audience had read Nancy Drew (and perhaps Trixie Belden) novels in their youth and had paid to see the mysteries; they wanted the play to maintain the spirit of Nancy Drew. They might have smiled readily at a respectable satire of their favorite sleuth, but would not have her (or them!) being ridiculed.

Trixie True, Teen Detective was not a commercial success, but it was a major undertaking that marks the first time Nancy played Broadway.

Nancy Drew: Girl Detective

In sharp contrast to Trixie True, the next adaptation of the series, produced by the prestigious Children's Theatre Company of Minneapolis, dealt with the problem of depicting a familiar heroine like Nancy by keeping her essence intact. According to the play program, director Alan Shorter and playwright Marisha Chamberlain worked from a simple, effective premise: "Stay faithful to the characters and situations from the books, and the actions of the characters on stage will define themselves." One critic added, "Chamberlain solved the problem by placing her tongue firmly in cheek and giving us a mystery that [was] equal parts homage to and gentle spoof of the Nancy Drew formula." As a result, Nancy Drew: Girl Detective, which ran from February 14 to April 8, 1990, was both a critical and a commercial success.

The ninety-minute play had a plot based primarily on The Clue of the Dancing Puppet (1962) and characters drawn from The Mystery at Lilac Inn (1930, revised 1961). It featured a professional cast of twenty-six members, with Annie Enneking in the title role of Nancy Drew.

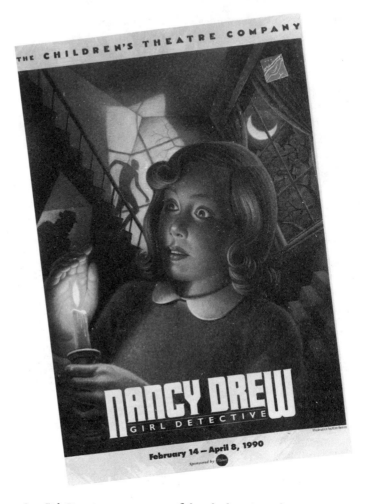

The Children's Theatre Company of Minneapolis designed this program for its production of *Nancy Drew: Girl Detective.*

In *Girl Detective,* a troupe of local thespians known as the Footlighters are using the estate of the late Mr. Van Pelt for their summer-stock fare. The problem? Life-size puppets are appearing on the lawn at night. The Spencers, who run the theater, believe one of the apparitions, the young ballerina, is the ghost of their deceased daughter.

Hamilton Spencer calls in Nancy to investigate, and along with Bess and George, she goes undercover as a scene painter. Soon, another tragedy occurs: priceless diamonds are stolen from the Spencers' surviving daughter, Emily, on the eve of her eighteenth birthday. The plot thickens, and the villains spur chaos, but Nancy and friends valiantly persevere, and in the end, justice reigns supreme.

The Children's Theatre Company, the leading theater for young people in North America, designed sets and costumes that captured the cinematic, 1940s ambience of the plot. Nancy even drove a custom-designed blue roadster.

During the run of *Girl Detective*, Peter Vaughan of the *Star Tribune* asked Minneapolis notables for childhood memories of Nancy Drew. Mary Kelley Leer, owner of Ruby's Cabaret, replied, "There was a big sandbar at the southwest corner of [Lake Harriet] with a big rain sewer. We would pack our provisions . . . and go into the sewers as deep as we could . . . so we could read Nancy Drew mysteries. It was an adventure of our own that added to the intrigue in this dark, dank place. We would huddle around and read and wait to see who could last. Eventually, one of us ran screaming from the sewer."

It is this type of innocent yet very real "eerie but fun" feeling that the play version of *Nancy Drew: Girl Detective* captured for her longtime fans.

Nancy Drew: Girl Detective featured Annie Enneking as Nancy (center), Lila Glasoe as Bess (left), and Raina Brody as George. (The Children's Theatre Company)

No doubt Carolyn Keene would have given Girl Detective a standing ovation.

Nancy Drew: Girl Detective
Horizon's Theatre, Washington, D.C.

In June 1991 Marisha Chamberlain's Girl Detective was revived at the Marvin Center, George Washington University. This time it sported a new cast and new director (Leslie B. Jacobson) and subsequently its own style. Nancy Drew was portrayed by Jane Beard, who was lauded for her believable, elegant performance.

Throughout the production, Nancy was dressed in 1930s style, down to her green-and-black dotted silk dress with white gloves. Costume designer William Pucilowsky, esteemed for his prior work with the Washington Stage Guild, decked out the female cast members in period playsuits, and the evildoers were dressed in properly cartoonish attire.

Like the premier production of the Children's Theatre Company in Minneapolis, the Horizon's Theatre's tongue-in-cheek interpretation of Nancy maintained the allure of the sleuth and the stories her fans loved as children. The play enjoyed a successful run. As Washington Post critic Lloyd Rose noted: "Its wackiness is poetic, dreamy, kind of touching. We see Nancy through her magic glasses."

Nancy Drew, Girl Detective at the Horizon's Theatre
Marvin Center, George Washington University, Washington, D.C.

Written by Marisha Chamberlain. Directed by Leslie B. Jacobson.
Set: Carl F. Gudenius; Costumes: William Pucilowsky;
Lights: Daniel MacLean Wagner; Music: John A. Ward.
Cast: Eamon Hunt, Arnie Stenseth, Julie Bayer, Ginger Moss, Adriana Wos, Jane Beard, Dariush Kashani, Lisa Lias, Steven Dawn, Richie Porter, Ed Johnson, Mary Woods, John Lescault, Michael Willis, John Gerken, Pamela Hoffman, Bahar Mikhak, Kathleen Strouse.

Repertory Productions

Farah's Price Guide (1989) briefly mentions three other plays inspired by Nancy Drew. The first is the Amherst Feminist Repertory Company's New York production of *Bonnie Keane, Girl Sleuth*, written by Eileen Stewart and Sarah Alleman.

Chris Steinbrunner's column in *Ellery Queen Mystery Magazine* (May 1978) described one of the songs, "Looking for Clues," as "a superb evoking of all the incidents and quests of this literary school, an innocent world of lilac inns and whispering statues now seemingly as tamed and gone as its attic secrets."

The second reference in *Farah's Price Guide* is to *The Clue in the Old Birdbath*, staged by the At the Foot of the Mountain players at the Southern Theater in Minneapolis from January 1 to 9, 1985. The musical was publicized as an "affectionate feminist satire" on Nancy Drew, with a script by Kate Kasten and Sandra de Helen, music and lyrics by Paul Boesing.

The third play (also staged in Minneapolis) was called *The Mystery of the Tattered Trunk*. It was produced by the Children's Theatre Company and ran from February 8 to April 12, 1985. In *Arts Pages*, reviewer Robert Collins explained that the plot revolves around an eighteen-year-old sleuth named Ms. McGrew who tries to track down "who's blackmailing whom on board the S.S. *Lavinia* on its maiden voyage from England to America in 1928." Collins added that the associate artistic director of the theater, Wendy Lehr, had hoped to adapt an actual Nancy Drew mystery but ran into problems because the series was then changing publishers.

The Nancy Drew Ballet

The first full-scale Nancy Drew ballet premiered on March 16, 1990, at the Civic Theater in Akron, Ohio. It featured thirty-eight young, talented dancers of the Cuyahoga Valley Youth Ballet in an adaptation of volume #32, *The Scarlet Slipper Mystery* (1954). The story ballet was staged by New York choreographer Michael Vernon; the libretto was adapted by artistic director Nan Klinger and board member Kathy Antonucci.

Nancy Drew's Scarlet Slipper Mystery
Cuyahoga Valley Youth Ballet, Civic Theater of Akron, Ohio
Choreographer: Michael Vernon. Libretto: Nan Klinger and Kathy Antonucci
Featured cast members: Piper Murray (Nancy Drew); Tecca Harris (George Fayne);
Corrie Wickland (Bess Marvin); Brian Murphy (Ned Nickerson);
Tiffany Kmet (prima ballerina); Julie Ports (kidnapper) and Gary Lenington (kidnapper).

The *Cleveland Plain Dealer* (March 15, 1990) reported that Nancy Drew was played by seventeen-year-old Piper Murray, who, like most of the other cast members, had read all the Drew books, watched the television shows, and thought Nancy Drew was a "true heroine." In that article, Murray stated, "Nancy Drew is like a supergirl . . . a know-it-all teenager and a real practical person."

The fact that the adaptation was brought to life entirely by teens close to Nancy Drew's age added a refreshing, innocent dimension to the show.

Scarlet Slipper centered on the plight of a renowned ballerina who, while wearing her red tap shoes, was kidnapped by the dastardly Mr. and Mrs. Judson. The plot led Nancy and friends to an airport, a ballet studio, and a theater stage, all the while dancing to the fast-paced music of George Gershwin. "Embraceable You" was the ballerina's theme, and "Strike Up the Band" was the grand finale. Costumes and sets reflected styles of the 1940s—the preferred period for many of the Nancy Drew productions.

Nancy Drew and the Clues: The Band

One of Nancy's most unusual spin-offs was in the rock music branch of the performing arts—a band in the mid-1980s named Nancy Drew and The Clues. According to Tom Graphia (*Daily News*, February 21, 1985), the group mixed "high energy dance music with playful audience interaction."

The band included Cheryl Walter on bass, Susan "S.K." Skywalker on keyboards and guitar, Cheryl Post on drums, Rick Dasher on guitar, and Eddie Robertson on keyboards and trumpet.

Information about this presumably short-lived band is particularly elusive.

Nancy Drew Collectibles: The Secrets in Your Dusty Old Attic

The Evolution of the Nancy Drew Collectibles Market

Like any other character who has captured the hearts of the populace, Nancy Drew has triggered the appearance of a respectable number of items that are now considered collectibles. Statistically, Nancy Drew mysteries are the number one choice among collectors of girls' series books, and because of the series' extended publishing history, fans spanning four generations are eagerly amassing pre-1962, dust-jacketed volumes and limited-run products like the Nancy Drew board game, doll, and lunch box. As can be expected, such collectibles are increasing in price as their availability decreases. First editions of *The Secret of the Old Clock* (1930), which originally sold for fifty cents, now command up to $500 on the open market, and a recent auction for the Nancy Drew Mystery Board Game called for a minimum bid of $125! Such escalated prices are the exception, however, and many Nancy Drew collectibles can still be purchased for less than $40.

Equally important, Nancy is just as popular now as she was in 1930; incredibly, her books continue to sell briskly. This indicates that collectors can find a long-lasting, rewarding, and versatile hobby in America's best-known teenage sleuth. New titles and products will no doubt become the memorabilia of tomorrow, and the oldest, rarest collectibles will continue to rise in value.

This Nancy Drew game board, produced by Parker Brothers in the late 1950s, is a favorite with collectors. (Photo by Joe Lance)

Until fairly recently, children's series books were not considered viable items in America's nostalgia market, nor were Drew titles included on lists of cherished literature prepared by traditional children's book societies. Books like *The Mystery at Lilac Inn* never made number one on any recommended reading lists.

For decades, Nancy Drew and the rest of the "fifty-cent" juvenile books introduced in the first third of the twentieth century were maligned by many librarians, teachers, and social reformers; elitist book collectors also scoffed. The first group labeled the authors of series books "hack writers," and they were eager to point out that the adventures, although engaging to young readers, lacked the literary merit of such stories as *Black Beauty* or *Little Women*. Specialty book collecting societies agreed with these sentiments and also refused to acknowledge the influx of "cheap" children's books as noteworthy.

Over the years, the "fifty-cent" heroes and heroines were even charged with permanently damaging the souls and minds of innocent youth! Former chief executive of the Boy Scouts of America, Franklin K. Mathiews, summed up the feelings of anti-series-book extremists in his scathing article, "Blowing Out the Boys' Brains" (*Outlook*, November 1914): "Story books of the right sort stimulate and conserve this noble facility [imagination], while those of a cheaper sort, by over-stimulation, debauch and vitiate, as brain and body are debauched and destroyed by strong drink." When Nancy Drew entered the scene in 1930, she represented double jeopardy to such critics. Nancy was a series-book sleuth who happened to be a girl. And girls definitely shouldn't have been acting so "foolhardy."

So Nancy Drew and her thrill-seeking colleagues made their debut amid a flurry of adult scorn. In spite of this, or perhaps because of it, boys and girls loved the superhuman exploits portrayed in the series books. According to the 1931 U.S. biennial census of book manufacturers, the greatest percentage of the twenty-two million juvenile books produced that year were "fifty-centers." The market skyrocketed in the 1930s, and Nancy Drew quickly moved to the front of the pack, her sales eventually surpassing favorites like The Hardy Boys, Rover Boys, Bomba, and The Bobbsey Twins.

Still, old attitudes die hard, and in this case bad press had enough impact to keep juvenile series books in check. Once read, these used texts were usually relegated to dusty shelves at thrift shops.

Fortunately for series-book enthusiasts, nostalgia and foresight gradually overcame cultural prejudice.

Development of Series-Book Organizations: Fans and Fanzines

During the 1950s and '60s, when collectors began to show a serious interest in fifty-cent juvenilia, they found themselves in a quandary. There were societies for bottle collecting, plate collecting, furniture collecting, and traditional children's book collecting—but there was no base for series-book collecting.

The market remained small and fragmented for many years. The publication *Dime Novel Round-Up* (instituted in the 1930s) was still thriving, but its scope was limited primarily to the collection of boys' dime novels. Therefore, a handful of earnest series-book collectors existed in a geographical vacuum; organized trading and buying was rare, and guidelines for identifying and rating books and merchandise were virtually nonexistent. But as time wore on, more and more adults who grew up with Nancy Drew and her fictional contemporaries were drawn back to the beautiful dust jackets and the exciting stories that had inspired them in their youth. Those who still had their original copies of blue Nancys, red Hardys, and beige Horatio Algers could not bear to give them away. They grew tired of being belittled for their interest in what hardliners called "trash" literature, for preferring adventure books to highbrow material. Forward-looking collectors also realized that the "fifty-center" boom of the twentieth century represented an important, potentially profitable landmark in publishing history.

Loyal fans who longed to share their enthusiasm with kindred spirits finally took matters into their own hands. Groups and fanzines focusing on boys' series books and story papers were first on the scene. Specialty newsletters began to circulate across the country. In 1961 the Horatio Alger Society was founded, followed by the Popular Culture Association, American Culture Association's Division of Dime Novels, Series Books and Pulp Collectors, Series Book Collectors' Society, and others. The *Mystery & Adventure Series Review* debuted in 1974.

Through these sources, fans of boys' series books and story magazines were able to find each other, share views, purchase books, and network. But collectors of girls' series books had yet to mobilize.

There was a brief flurry of activity in 1973 when two sisters from San Francisco interested in starting a Nancy Drew club placed ads in the local newspapers calling for Nancy Drew fans. Initially the ads generated about forty replies, and a group started meeting informally to trade books and trivia, view the Nancy Drew movies, and so on. Although the regional club eventually disbanded, national interest in Nancy Drew as a pop culture figure did not.

In 1975 articles acknowledging Nancy Drew (and other Stratemeyer Syndicate–generated series) as one of the up-and-coming trends in the nostalgia market appeared regularly in publications like *A. B. Bookman*, *The Book Collector*, and *Hobbies* magazine. In *The Antiques Journal* (July 1975), Dr. Fred Davis, then a sociologist at the University of California, related the nostalgia and renewed interest in Nancy to the turmoil of the 1960s. Davis theorized that adults seeking anchor points for stability were being drawn back to the famous sleuth because, in spite of her adventures, "Nancy Drew represents a surprisingly secure world."

The word was out that Nancy Drew and Nancy Drew collectibles would be around for a long time. Early titles that proprietors had stashed away in the back of their second-hand stores were moved to the front, sporting heftier price tags. In 1978 the first girls' series bibliography was published by the Children's Literature Research Collections (Hess Collection) based at the University of Minnesota library, and Nancy Drew titles were duly represented. By the early 1980s, the future looked promising, with old favorites like Nancy, Judy Bolton, Cherry Ames, Penny Parker, and Beverly Gray finally getting respectable attention.

In January 1981, an avid collector named Gil O'Gara started a fanzine called *Yellowback Library* to foster communication among boys' pulp and series-book fans. As it turned out, girls' books also received a great deal of attention in *Yellowback*, and Nancy Drew was the subject of at least twenty different articles in the first years of publication. Finally, late in 1985, girls' book collectors created their own fanzine.

Three colleagues who had been exchanging information and books by mail decided to start an organization called the Society of Phantom Friends. The group, open to anyone over thirteen who reads and collects girls' series books, has grown into a major organization with a large membership.

Under the enthusiastic guidance of the organization's president and cofounder, Kate Emburg, the Phantoms publish a monthly newsletter called *The Whispered Watchword*, which features Nancy Drew in every single issue along with nostalgia pieces, convention updates, book reviews, buy/sell lists, and more. The Phantoms, and other similar societies, have helped promote interest in the girls' series field, and their publications and conferences have helped Nancy Drew collectors from all over the United States to share their knowledge and experiences.

One of the most important contributions to the Nancy Drew collectibles field was a technical guide to formats and titles that was self-published by researcher David Farah. The first edition appeared in 1985, and the book is continually updated. Additional studies of the Nancy Drew series soon followed, and an enormous amount of technical and biographical information is now available to collectors of Nancy Drew memorabilia.

Finally, late in 1985, the first "Series Book Collectors' Society 1985–1986 Membership Directory" was published by the Series Book Collectors' Society of Riverside, Rhode Island. Within months, fans of both boys' and girls' series books were communicating with each other in record numbers, and the juvenile nostalgia market truly started to thrive.

Ironically, there is no official Nancy Drew fan club for the series' target audience, children aged eight to twelve! There almost was, however. In 1980, shortly after Simon & Schuster introduced the first paperback Wanderer editions (beginning with Nancy Drew Mystery Story #57), an ad inside the books announced an official Nancy Drew/Hardy Boys Fan Club: "Be the first in your neighborhood to find out about the newest ad-

August 1990   .   Number 74

Yellowback Library

BIG NEWS!
"Lost" Stratemeyer
Syndicate Series
Rediscovered!

Mildred Wirt Benson
Attends Series
Book Convention!

Plus: Hardy Boys,
Irving Crump,
News, Reviews, and
Lots of Ads!

Specialty publications such as *Yellowback Library* and *The Whispered Watchword* have been instrumental in organizing the Nancy Drew nostalgia market.

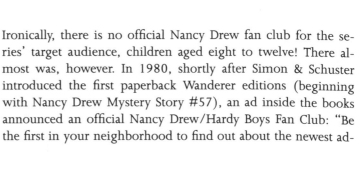

ventures of Nancy, Frank, and Joe in the *Nancy Drew/Hardy Boys Mystery Reporter.*" According to *Farah's Price Guide* (1989), a follow-up four-page flyer with a fan club membership card was indeed issued, in limited quantities, in 1980. The flyer advertised the changing look and focus of the Nancy Drew and Hardy Boys books and included an interview with "Carolyn Keene." In 1981 Simon & Schuster issued a second edition of the flyer, this time featuring an exclusive sneak preview of the latest Hardy Boys mystery. That is the last official fan club publication known to exist.

In fall 1986, shortly after the Nancy Drew Files series was launched, *Americana* magazine ran an article about a proposed Nancy Drew River Heights, USA fashion collection. At that time, a related fan club and publication for teens called Nancy Drew's River Heights Country Club was allegedly being formed to dispense tips on health, beauty, and dating for preteens. Enthusiasm was high among fans, young and old, for these two innovative concepts, but unfortunately, neither the fashion line nor the preteen fan club ever surfaced.

According to Simon & Schuster's executive editor Anne Greenberg, the publisher did not receive sufficient responses from interested young fans to continue with a full-blown fan club, and there are no plans to start another in the near future.

The Present State of the Nancy Drew Market

Today, children's series books and their accompanying memorabilia are acknowledged as a bona fide genre in the nostalgia field. Through the hard work and loyalty of fans, the blond-haired sleuth who seems to have and do it all is a major player on the market.

In *Yellowback Library's* 1990–1991 *Directory of Series Book Collectors,* more collectors cited Nancy Drew on their "want" lists than any other girls' series heroine. Publisher Gil O'Gara summarized current trends: "The market for series books has proven to be strong and steady. Post World War II books are increasingin demand, theoretically because of the number of baby boomers entering the ranks of the hobby. The top five collectible series appear to be the Hardy Boys, Nancy Drew, Rick Brant, Tom Swift and Judy Bolton. Girls' series are gaining in interest and the male segment of the collecting community, and the public at large, is becoming more and more aware of the variety of girls' fiction on the market." According to O'Gara, the increase in publicity and bibliographic information for girls' series generates enthusiasm and competition for the same authors and titles.

This is certainly true in the case of Nancy Drew collectibles, as an unprecedented number of fans are now vying for a piece of the literary pie. Statistics and theories aside, the truest test of market growth can be experienced closer to home. It wasn't long ago that one could stroll through an old-book store or browse the racks at a flea market and find any number of Drew titles being sold for fifty to seventy-five cents. Today, visitors to those same haunts will find Nancy Drew books (along with those of her pals, the Hardy Boys) neatly piled apart from the rest of the series books, commanding higher prices and inciting more competition among buyers than an after-Christmas sale at Bloomingdale's.

At an antique shop in New Jersey, an unsuspecting owner recently set outside the store a box of twenty-five mint-condition Nancy Drew titles from the 1940s for the price of $1.50 per book. Within minutes, a crowd of wild-eyed buyers swarmed into the area, fighting (verbally, of course) for the books. The first to reach the proprietor walked away with the prize, but before this buyer got to the parking lot she had turned around and sold them for $5.00 each to another woman, who didn't even blink at the arrangement. When a passerby asked the second buyer why she so anxiously spent her money on "dusty old books" in lieu of the fine antiques available inside the store, she replied, "I read all the Nancy Drews when I was a girl. She was a great inspiration to me and I want to have her, and all those books, back again."

Although some people are solely interested in economic aspects, the vast majority of Nancy Drew collectors are *also* Nancy Drew fans who readily admit that reading those books reminds them of a time when they were inspired to be all they could be . . . to take on new challenges . . . to dream of *being* their favorite quintessential American heroine.

One Nancy Drew fan, Victoria Broadhurst, reports that her custom-made license plate draws attention and waves from fellow Nancy Drew enthusiasts when she travels the highways. (V. Broadhurst)

The range of Nancy Drew collectibles is decidedly vast, yet not as all-encompassing as, for example, that of Star Trek or Disney memorabilia. Drew items continue to be within the financial reach of the general population. It is enlightening to know that in a world traditionally dominated by a handful of collectors carrying off millions of dollars of Louis XIV furniture and Chippendale highboys, collecting series books can be a satisfying and affordable hobby for the average consumer. And the fact that Nancy Drew's new adventures are still selling well in bookstores is testimony to the theory that this market is not a fly-by-night fad. It will be around for a long time.

Whether you remember reading the blue Nancys, yellow Nancys, or multicolored library editions, chances are you can find them again—perhaps even in your own dusty old attic—soon after you make your transition from "fan" to serious collector.

Building a Collection

If you are interested in starting a Nancy Drew collection, your first step is to become familiar with the types of books and products on the market. While it is impossible to list the price and description of every Nancy Drew collectible, this book provides a basic description of the different categories of collectibles and a sampling of the most unusual or popular items. There is also a section outlining where and how to acquire collectibles and a system for keeping track of your collection.

Categories of Nancy Drew Collectibles

Nancy Drew collectibles can be divided into seven major categories:

1. **Original Texts: The Blue Nancys.** The most popular text collectibles are the first thirty-eight titles released by Grosset & Dunlap in dust-jacketed, hardcover form between 1930 and 1961. These incorporate original text versions (and copyright dates), from *The Secret of the Old Clock* through *The Mystery of the Fire Dragon*, and are known in the business as the "blue Nancys" for the color of their covers. Of these, the first twenty-seven titles (the majority of which were written by Mildred Wirt Benson under the Carolyn Keene name and illustrated by Russell H. Tandy) command especially high prices. Most prized, and expensive, are the early printings of the first three Nancy Drew mysteries released as test-marketed volumes in 1930 and 1931.

2. **The Yellow Nancys**. In the 1960s Grosset & Dunlap did away with dust jackets and blue covers and introduced the yellow-spine picture-cover format. Books produced in this format include new titles from volumes #39 to #56, *The Clue of the Dancing Puppet* (1962) through *The Thirteenth Pearl* (1979), along with revised volumes #1 through #38. Beginning in 1962, the original Drews were re-released, bearing updated copyright dates and revised texts and formats. These volumes marked a major change in Nancy and company, especially in the text itself, where popular culture demanded the deletion of racial and professional stereotypes, outdated phrases, and outmoded conveniences. In addition, almost all the original Russell Tandy covers were redone by Bill Gillies and Rudy Nappi, who changed Nancy Drew's look for a new generation.

During this transition, a limited supply of yellow-spine picture covers were released with new art and the *original* texts. These are especially sought-after by collectors.

3. **Special text releases and foreign editions.** Numerous special editions were published by Grosset & Dunlap over the years, including the "Double Edition," "Triple Edition," Cameo Editions, and Nancy Drew Picture Books. Many fans will also recall *The Nancy Drew Cookbook*. Released in 1973, this theme-oriented cooking guide was a hit with fans and merited a number of reprints. Other examples that fall into this category are foreign releases, library-bound editions, and book club releases, which come in myriad formats and cover colors.

4. **Products and games inspired by the series.** This category consists of items that were available to the public for limited periods, such as the Nancy Drew Jigsaw Puzzle and Madame Alexander Nancy Drew Doll, which are covered in more detail in chapter 14.

Aside from first-edition volumes of the series, Nancy Drew spin-off products and games are the most sought-after collectibles. They are sometimes advertised for sale in the fanzines, but it is more common for collectors to locate them on their own at estate sales and flea markets. Considering Nancy's popularity, the range of series-related products is relatively small. Her counterparts, the Hardy Boys, inspired more items than Nancy Drew. This may be due in part to the stringent guide-

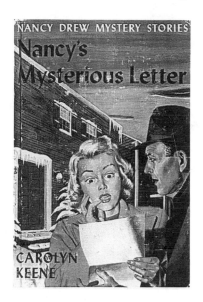

Copyright, 1932, by
GROSSET & DUNLAP, INC.

All Rights Reserved

Nancy's Mysterious Letter

Grosset & Dunlap issued several "odd formats" in limited supply during the transition from blue hardcovers with dust jackets to yellow picture covers in the early 1960s. This yellow volume of *Nancy's Mysterious Letter* includes the revised cover art by Bill Gillies. The text and frontispiece, however, are the 1932 originals. This edition is worth $10 to $15 in very good condition. (Simon & Schuster)

Through the decades, a number of different merchandisers handled the Nancy Drew line. In the late 1950s, around the time the Parker Brothers Nancy Drew game appeared, the William C. Erskine agency of New York City used Nancy Drew's popularity to attract new clients. This ad appeared in *Playthings*, July 1956.

Opposite page: Articles about Nancy Drew have appeared in newspapers and major magazines across America. Tracking down such material is all part of the fun of collecting Nancy Drew memorabilia.

lines imposed by Harriet S. Adams. Few products met her approval.

5. **Stage and screen memorabilia and related promotional items.** These include authentic memorabilia and promotional items from the 1938 to 1939 Nancy Drew movies starring Bonita Granville as Nancy and Frankie Thomas as Ted (not Ned), along with items related to the 1970s television show starring Pamela Sue Martin.

Authentic promotional posters, print ads, programs, publicity stills, and scripts from the plays and ballets inspired by Nancy Drew are also popular collectibles.

6. **Items and documents related to the actual publication of the series.** This, the most diverse of the seven categories, covers a broad spectrum of collectibles and is therefore the hardest in which to assign accurate values. It encompasses items associated with the technical production of the series, such as letters, contracts, autographs of esteemed "Carolyn Keenes," original artwork, and draft designs by Nancy Drew cover artists. (Particularly hard to find is correspondence mentioning the series addressed to or from Edward Stratemeyer or Harriet S. Adams.)

One lucky collector has acquired the typewriter Mildred Benson used to write the first Nancy Drew manuscript, but such items are rarely in circulation. When serious collectors grab hold of such prizes, they are not inclined to let them go. On the other hand, new memorabilia seems to surface every year and many collectibles await discovery.

7. **The new collectibles.** These include titles now being released by Simon & Schuster in the Nancy Drew Files (young adult version) format and the paperback Nancy Drew Mystery Stories. There are also a number of spin-off series such as River Heights USA, The Nancy Drew & Hardy Boys SuperMysteries, Be a Detective Mystery Stories, and others. These contemporary titles—especially the first printings—eventually might reach the status of collectibles, so acquiring them now could pay off later.

The category of new collectibles also extends to authorized facsimile editions. In 1992 Applewood Books of Bedford, Massachusetts, released facsimile editions of the first three Nancy Drew mysteries (and the Hardy Boys). These beautifully

Negro Stereotypes in Children's Literature: The Case of Nancy Drew

ENTERTAINMENT FOR MEN

PLAYBOY

NEIMAN PAINTS
ELVIS PRESLEY!
YOUR OWN
TEAR-OUT

CARL SAGAN
PARANORM

JULY 1978 • $2.00

TV'S
NCY DREW
UNDRAPED

The Real-Life Heroine Who Wrote Nancy Drew

OINES

men, success, and Nancy Drew

at makes a heroine in 1930—or
ains, guts, and a touch of class

FRANCES FITZGERALD

Not all mythical figures wear togas,
and Carl Gustav Jung did not finish the job of cataloging all the ar-
chetypes of human existence. There
re modern characters who loom far larger in
he collective unconscious than any Greek
deity—at least to judge from the sale of
books. Take the Gothic heroine for example.
If you've never read a Gothic novel, think of
Jane Eyre and forget (as you surely have) the
ending. A beautiful dark young woman, orphaned at birth but educated—to gentility,
goes off to work as a governess in a gloomy
castle. There are skeletons in the cellar and
half-naked women raving upstairs. It rains a
lot, and the only oth—
lover. Finally, just
set-up nobleman re
fate worse than de
ment, and the need
On the other ha
It can
have
novel
nive
fifty
som
Dr
Ad
an

she puts on the occasional p
shorts, but never, *never* has s
blue jeans, minis, or gran
lives in what seems to be a w
a small Middle Western city
a nice, clean, friendly plac
farmland and wooded lake
father, Carson Drew, is a
of this town, a distinguish
and former district attorn
an independent professio
so; enough to give Nancy financial security
well as impeccable social credentials. I
but only in part

Children's Book Scene

EDITED BY DIANE ROBACK

**NANCY DREW:
Then and Now**

The perennially popula
is being repac

Nancy Drew's New Loo'

other children, his
died when Nancy was three.
and intelligent, Car-

**Of clues, kisses, and childho
memories: Nancy Drew revisi**

• by Joanne Furtak, 21, Hamden, Conn. •

**Their
Success Is
No Mystery**

The author tells
why Nancy Drew
and the
Hardy Boys
have delighted
three generations
and inspired
a TV series

number is almo
population of this country ove
eight. It surely exceeds the number of females
whose parents could have afforded to buy
them a hardcover mystery when they were
eight, nine, or ten years old. Such popularity
over fifty years calls into question the very
notion of a "generation gap"—at least as if
applies to girls of about that age.
Of course, some girls (some boys as well)
have read the Nancy Drew books mere-
of a superbly f   deeper at-

house—no on
housekeeper called Hannah G
Gruen is very much a part of the family. A
"motherly" woman of a certain age, she
keeps the home fires burning with domestic
warmth. She dotes on Nancy and looks up to
her. Nancy thus has a "mother" who is no rival for her father's affections and no threat to
her status in the house. She has sex aside
all the advantages of being a wife and a
daughter with none of the corresponding dis-
She lives in an Oedipal dream

In honor of Nancy Drew's hundredth mystery in 1991, Simon & Schuster issued a special anniversary edition, *A Secret in Time*, which brought back the famous timepiece from volume #1, *The Secret of the Old Clock*. This edition is one example of the "new collectibles" sought after by fans. (Simon & Schuster)

bound, dust-jacketed reproductions feature the original text (and dust-jacket art) and include rare interior illustrations that most contemporary fans have never seen. Each book includes a preface by a best-selling mystery author: Sara Paretsky in *The Secret of the Old Clock*, Nancy Pickard in *The Hidden Staircase*, and P. M. Carlson in *The Bungalow Mystery*.

Diehard Drew fans also collect published material about Nancy Drew and the golden age of the Stratemeyer Syndicate in the form of magazine and newspaper articles. Admittedly, the monetary value of such literature is low to nil; however, it adds to the enjoyment of the collecting experience. Coverage of Nancy Drew began in 1930 when she made her debut, and has since surfaced in virtually every major American newspaper and antique periodical, along with more than five hundred specialty and mass-market publications, including *Publishers Weekly, Woman's Day, Seventeen, McCall's, Library Journal, Newsweek, Fortune,* and even *Playboy*. Nancy Drew is now a household name, and collectors seeking in-depth information about her will never run out of sources! You can use the Select Bibliography in the back of this book as a starting point.

The Next Step: Setting a Goal

Now that you have an idea of the numerous types of Nancy Drew books available, you are probably anxious to assemble your own collection. But don't be too anxious. Always remember to think before you buy. Any experienced series-book collector will tell you that it is easy to get carried away with enthusiasm and start buying every title you see. This often leads to a shelf full of rejects (items not suitable for selling, trading, or appraising) and possibly hundreds of dollars in losses. Avoid this by setting a realistic collecting goal based on your personal preferences and your current financial resources.

If your immediate goal is to gather together every available Nancy Drew book and product, in all their various formats and incarnations, *and* you have an unlimited bank account, then you can stop reading this chapter right now. Secure copies of the series-book fanzines, get on the phone, and you'll have a mind-boggling collection in no time.

However, if you are an average-income consumer with strict spending limits, you'd be wise to tread a bit more carefully. It helps to decide on one particular Nancy Drew format and focus on obtaining titles in that category. For example, if you already own a few yellow picture-cover Nancy Drews, you can set a goal of acquiring all the volumes that were issued in that cover style. If you prefer the blue Nancys, you can aim for a complete set of those; if you can't bear anything less than dust-jacketed editions, begin there, and so on.

If you feel this approach is too limiting, then you can simply start out by purchasing one of each volume in the series, regardless of format, until you have a complete set. This works especially well if you are a garage sale or flea market enthusiast—at these places you never know what will turn up. Setting a specific goal makes the acquisition process go more smoothly and allows you to gradually build up an impressive collection.

When it comes to Nancy Drew items such as the board game or lunch box, the rules are a bit different. Since these products are so hard to find, make acquiring them a priority goal from day one if they interest you. Your challenge here is not to guard against overenthusiasm, but instead to avoid being overcharged for your purchases. The best way to get a fair price is to learn as much as possible about the current value of Nancy Drew collectibles before you say, "I'll take it."

A Special Word About Reproductions

Advanced technology has made laser-printed color copies of the original dust jackets and 1930s film posters increasingly popular. Occasionally, however, these are offered for sale as "originals" at escalated prices. Before you pay a high price for a rare original, make sure you're getting the real thing.

How to Find Nancy Drew Collectibles

Armed with newfound knowledge and a pocketful of cash, you are ready to venture out into the world of collecting. Where to begin? You have a variety of choices.

The most active venue for Drew materials is the mail, through which juvenile series fans and dealers "in the know" buy, sell, and trade on a regular basis. As already mentioned, the fanzines are one source for buying through the mail, and some of them publish membership directories. See the Directory of Sources on page 147.

Rummage sales, garage sales, and flea markets are also great reservoirs of unexpected finds. There is something very exciting about getting to one of these events early and searching through musty boxes for a coveted title or item. Sometimes you find it, sometimes you don't. But generally, the prices at such markets are hard to beat.

Used-book stores are always worth investigating. If you find that a store in your area handles children's titles, make it your business to leave your card or name and a list of the books you are looking for. Since the inventory in used-book stores changes frequently, the proprietor should be aware of your interest. This way, there's a good chance he or she will give you a call if a truckful of dust-jacketed Nancy Drew books arrive, before another fan gets to them.

One dealer and collector, Mike DeBaptiste, finds that the best way to get books is to advertise in local newspapers. In a 1990 article in The Whispered Watchword, Mike advised collectors to run ads in the classified section for a week or two at a time. His ads always read: NANCY DREW BOOKS WANTED. TOP PRICE PAID, followed by his phone number. Since Nancy Drew is so well known, he always gets a large response. When people call, he asks specific questions about the books, then decides whether or not to pursue the sale.

Last is word-of-mouth advertising. Tell everyone you know that you are looking for Nancy Drew titles and before long you will be getting responses and referrals.

Given these alternatives, ambitious people can assemble a basic collection in a relatively short time—without mortgaging their house to do so. Just remember to familiarize yourself with the market first, and always think before you buy.

Directory of Sources

Specialty Publications and Organizations

The Whispered Watchword is a monthly publication of the Society of Phantom Friends, an organization for girls' series-book collectors age thirteen and older. Yearly membership, which costs $25, includes the fanzine, which offers articles on all facets of collecting and buy/sell/trade lists. Nancy Drew is featured in every issue. The Phantoms also sponsor an annual conference and regional meetings and offer a membership directory. For information write Kate Emburg, President, 4100 Cornelia Way, North Highlands, California 95660.

Yellowback Library is a monthly magazine for the collector, dealer, and enthusiast of juvenile series books, dime novels, and related literature. Regular features include buy/sell/trade ads, in-depth interviews and articles, hobby news, and reviews of other publications in the field. The publisher and editor is Gil O'Gara. Subscriptions cost $24 per year; $12 for six issues. Write to *Yellowback Library*, P.O. Box 36172, Des Moines, Iowa 50315 or call 515-287-0404.

Martha's KidLit Newsletter is a bimonthly guide for children's book collectors that includes feature stories about favorite authors, illustrators, classic titles, and series books, along with ads and reviews. Subscriptions cost $25 per year for six issues; $4.50 for single copies. Write to *Martha's KidLit Newsletter*, P.O. Box 1488, Ames, Iowa 50010.

Collectors' Guides

Farah's Price Guide to Nancy Drew Books and Collectibles, Ninth Edition, self-published by David Farah, 1992. Includes five hundred pages of information on Nancy Drew mysteries from 1930 to 1979. Two thousand format listings help date your books. Contains a complete price guide and costs $50 post paid. Order from David Farah, 3110 Park Newport, Apt. #412, Newport Beach, California 92660.

Girls' Series Companion, published by the Society of Phantom Friends. Detailed listings of all major girls' series books, past and present, with brief descriptions of each book, cross-referenced author/title guides; includes Nancy Drew, Cherry Ames, Judy Bolton, and hundreds of others. For information about the current edition and price, write to Kate Emburg, President, 4100 Cornelia Way, North Highlands, California 95660.

Further Reading

The Mystery of Nancy Drew: Girl Sleuth on the Couch by Betsy Caprio (Source Books, 1992). This illustrated, large-format softcover book ($14.95 post paid) uses Jungian themes, the original Nancy Drew texts, and firsthand accounts of the effects of the girl sleuth on people's lives and self-knowledge. Also available is a poster map of River Heights (black-and-white, 18" x 24"; $5 post paid) that depicts sights and scenes found in Nancy Drew mysteries; part of this map appears on pages 86–87. The book and map are available through Source Books, P.O. Box 794, Trabuco Canyon, California 92678.

The Secrets of the Stratemeyer Syndicate: Nancy Drew, the Hardy Boys, and the Million Dollar Fiction Factory by Carol Billman (New York: Ungar Publishing Co., 1986). This in-depth account of Stratemeyer operations and series books is out of print but available through most libraries.

The Lady Investigates: Women Detectives & Spies in Fiction by Patricia Craig and Mary Cadogan (New York: St. Martin's Press, 1981). Available through most libraries.

For other books and articles on Nancy Drew and the Stratemeyer Syndicate, see the Select Bibliography on page 176.

Clues for Dating and Rating Your Drew Books and Memorabilia

Since its premiere in 1930, *The Secret of the Old Clock* has gone through more than 150 printings. Nancy Drew was so popular with readers from the start that Grosset & Dunlap averaged two to three printings per year, with four trips back to press in 1932 and 1955. Most of the print runs incorporated a variation, however slight, in either binding, advertising text, endpapers, cover color, or paper. For example, in the first print run of 1943, a good-quality, off-white paper was used, and it maintained its fresh look over time. But by the end of 1943, the paper shortage triggered by World War II required publishers to cut back on quality. Any of the twenty-two Nancy Drew mysteries that survive from that era are noticeably more brittle and brown-toned. In fact, several volumes from the 1940s have a notice printed on the title page announcing that they were "produced under wartime conditions, in full compliance with government regulations for the conservation of paper."

There are at least eighty known variations of the dust-jacketed format of *Old Clock* alone, and another twenty or more in the yellow picture-cover format—and that is, of course, only one of the original fifty-six Nancy Drew mysteries. This makes the process of identifying the exact year your books were released, and then rating their worth, a major undertaking. Fortunately, *Farah's Price Guide to Nancy Drew Books and Collectibles* (see page 147) is available for serious collectors. However, if you are a novice or a curious owner of a few "blue tweed" Nancy Drews, there are certain characteristics you can check right now to estimate the age and value of your books.

Beware the Copyright Notice

Copyright notices in your books are *not an indication* of the year the book was printed. This is important to know because the print run of a Nancy Drew mystery has much bearing on its value. The copyright notice refers to the first year the book was registered with the Library of Congress. Usually, this date does not change until the book is revised enough to warrant a new copyright date. Therefore, your copy of *The Mystery at Lilac Inn* might state "©1930" but actually be from a 1950 printing. Keep that in mind when a bookstore owner tries to sell you an "authentic 1930 copy" of a Nancy Drew. Chances are, it wasn't printed in 1930. The first editions of the series are extremely distinctive and rare.

Copyright data can come in handy if you want to know whether a particular volume contains the original or the revised text. If your yellow picture-cover of *Old Clock* has a copyright date of 1959, then you are reading the revised version, not the 1930 text enjoyed by your grandmother. To make it simple, many of the yellow volumes have two dates printed on the copyright page. In this case you know you have a revised text.

If you are a fairly recent fan of Nancy Drew, it is worth your while to track down either yellow or blue hardcovers with pre-1959 copyright dates. To read the original volumes, with their old-fashioned ambience and little flaws, is a delightful experience.

Dust Jackets and Spine Colors

Nancy Drew titles were released by Grosset & Dunlap in blue hardcovers with full-color dust jackets from 1930 to 1961. These included volumes #1 through #56. The earlier printings, especially pre–World War II, had dust jackets with white spines and the books were relatively thick: if you close the book, the total width between the front cover and back cover should measure just over one inch. Later volumes had a wraparound jacket (portions of the dust-jacket illustration continued around to the spine of the book) and the pages were of thinner paper, reducing the overall depth to approximately three quarters of an inch. In general, books with white-spine dust jackets are worth more than those with wrap-spines.

Beneath the dust jackets, assorted blue tones were used on the covers: some were gray-blue, others dark blue, and so on. The most common is the medium blue tweed-type cover with dark blue lettering that was predominant in the 1950s.

Beginning in 1962, dust jackets were eliminated in favor of yellow picture-covers. The initial printings of the Nancy Drew "yellows" had a boxed picture on the back cover that showed Nancy peering out from behind a tree. Around 1966 this changed to a picture of Nancy looking through a magnifying glass. Many of the new Nancy Drews are also yellow-spined, but they have smooth, high-gloss picture covers and are easily distinguishable from the earlier versions, especially since the current versions include a drawing of a flashlight near the top of the front cover.

In 1979 Simon & Schuster started releasing new Nancy Drew mysteries in paperback format. The first printings of these volumes show a front color scene of Nancy surrounded by a half-moon "frame." The number of the volume is surrounded by a thick circle.

Identifying covers and dust jackets is one of the most daunting parts of collecting for beginners, but it quickly becomes enjoyable as you start to see your collections grow.

The Nancy Drew Silhouette

Studying the Nancy Drew silhouette on the cover of your blue hardcover is another quick way to establish the era of your volume. The 1930s silhouette showed Nancy with a magnifying glass, wearing high heels and a scarf. There is a shadow at her feet. This version appeared on the covers of books printed from 1932 to 1946. The second version of the silhouette eliminated the shadow at Nancy's feet, along with her scarf, and placed her in low pumps. This version appeared on books printed between 1947 and 1961.

If you have a blue volume with no silhouette on the cover, congratulations! You have acquired one of the first copies made, probably from one of the 1930 or 1931 printings (see page

THE CLUE
IN THE
JEWEL
BOX

CAROLYN
KEENE

A
*Nancy
Drew*
Mystery
Story...

GROSSET
& DUNLAP
20

Above is an example of a "white spine" from a 1943 dust jacket. (Simon & Schuster)

This Nancy Drew silhouette appeared on the blue hardcovers in the 1930s. (Simon & Schuster)

155 for a complete description of a first edition). No silhouette, just title and author, appeared on the covers of volumes #1 through #5, *The Secret of the Old Clock* through *The Secret at Shadow Ranch*. In very good condition, even without dust jackets, these thick blue volumes are worth between $50 and $300.

In general, a dust-jacketed copy of a Nancy Drew book is worth three to four times more than a nonjacketed volume. So stunning are the early dust jackets that many collectors frame their covers, or make color laser copies and use them as wall decorations.

Title Lettering

Remove the dust jacket if you have one, then study the cover. Are the letters printed in blue or orange? This is another clue to dating your books. The book title, author, and silhouette were printed in orange between 1930 and the first half of 1946. From the second half of 1946 through 1961, the publisher used blue ink for both the lettering and the silhouette.

Endpapers and Frontispieces

Open up your blue volume and look at the inside front cover. That side of the cover and its adjoining page are referred to as endpapers. Now keep turning until you see the first illustration in the book, which is called a frontispiece and is placed before the actual text begins.

Nancy Drew Mystery Stories frontispieces were printed on glossy paper until 1943. After that they appeared on plain, nonglossy paper. The illustrations on the endpapers (also known as "ends") and the frontispiece provide important historical data. What follows is a table to help determine the *approximate* time frame during which your book was printed.

Keep in mind this is only a general guide to formats. In some cases, Grosset & Dunlap used two or three different types of endpapers in the same year.

Table for Dating Your Blue Hardcover Drews

Print Run	Endpapers	Frontispiece
1930–1931	Blank (white); no picture.	Glossy paper
1932–1948	Orange silhouette; Nancy examining ground with quizzing glass, three girls nearby.	Glossy paper through part of 1943; after that, plain paper
1947–1948	Maroon illustration of two girls examining a note in an upstairs hallway.	Plain paper
1947–1952	Dark blue silhouette of Nancy examining ground with magnifying glass; three girls nearby.	Plain paper
1952–1958	Nancy stands behind a tree watching a man digging. Called "digger ends."	Plain paper
1958–1961	22 small illustrations of Nancy Drew covers on a blue background. Called "blue multiple scene."	Plain paper

The Monetary Value of Nancy Drew Mysteries: Volumes #1 Through #56

Now you have a general idea of the era in which your blue volumes were printed, but what are they worth? Prices vary widely. In general, a blue-tweed volume in very good condition with no dust jacket sells for $3 to $7, while the thicker volumes run $8 to $10. The yellow spine picture-covers range from $2 to $10, based on their rarity. Blue volumes with dust jackets are valued between $10 and $30, with scarce (and thicker) volumes worth much more.

Sometimes, an oddity in the text itself makes a particular book valuable. Early printings of volume #18, *The Mystery of the Moss-Covered Mansion* (copyright 1941) included a sentence on page 215 that said the name of the next book in the series was "The Quest of the Telltale Map." However, volume #19 turned out to be *The Quest of the Missing Map*. Copies of *Moss-Covered Mansion* with this error are worth $12 to $15, even without a dust jacket.

In the early printings of *The Clue in the Old Stagecoach* (copyright 1960), the name "Carolyn Keene" is printed twice on the spines of the yellow picture-covers. These volumes are worth $5 to $7.

Because there are so many variations like these, you'll have to do your own sleuthing to find out the exact worth of your collectibles!

Collectible Special Editions and Series Spin-offs

Along with the original Nancy Drew Mystery Stories, a number of one-of-a-kind editions were released over the years by Grosset & Dunlap, Simon & Schuster, Scholastic, and other publishers. The following list is just a sampling of the most popular text collectibles and their approximate values.

The "current value" shown after each description represents an average price derived from interviews with collectors, from ads that have appeared in fanzines, and from personal purchasing experiences. In all cases, the current value is based on books in very good (or excellent) condition.

The Nancy Drew Cookbook

The first edition of *The Nancy Drew Cookbook: Clues to Good Cooking* by Carolyn Keene was released in 1973 by Grosset & Dunlap. It had a yellow picture-cover format (no dust jacket) and 159

Outside:

(Note: This is a description of the book without the dust jacket.)

- Front cover: Gray-blue hardcover.

- Printing on front cover: Orange type outlined in dark blue that reads "The Secret of the Old Clock/Carolyn Keene." There is no silhouette on the front cover.

- Spine: Dark blue printing listing title, author, and publisher.

Inside:

- Endpapers: Blank (white).

- Illustrations: One glossy frontispiece and three additional glossy internal illustrations, all designed by Russell Tandy.

- Title page: Includes the following information: Nancy Drew Mystery Stories (underlined), title, author, names of Nancy Drew volumes #2 and #3 (The Hidden Staircase and The Bungalow Mystery); the phrase "Illustrated by Russell H. Tandy"; publisher identification.

- Copyright page: A box positioned toward the top of the page contains the following information (see above): "NANCY DREW MYSTERY STORIES/By CAROLYN KEENE/ 12mo. Cloth./Illustrated." Lists first three Nancy Drew mysteries only, along with publisher identification. A line below the box reads: "Copyright, 1930, by GROSSET & DUNLAP, Inc."

- Back pages: Include numerous ads for other series, including The Hardy Boys titles for volumes #1 through #8; Ted Scott Flying Stories volumes #1 through #11; Famous Rover Boys volumes #1 through #30; Don Sturdy volumes #1 through #9; and Radio Boys volumes #1 through #12. Two blank pages follow these ads.

Current value: Without dust jacket, $150 to $250; with dust jacket, $500.

**NANCY DREW
MYSTERY STORIES**

By CAROLYN KEENE

12mo.   Cloth.   Illustrated.

The Secret of the Old Clock
The Hidden Staircase
The Bungalow Mystery

(Other volumes in preparation)

GROSSET & DUNLAP, PUBLISHERS, NEW YORK

Copyright, 1930, by
GROSSET & DUNLAP, Inc.

pages. The cookbook sold exceedingly well and was reprinted several times.

In keeping with the Nancy Drew theme, almost every dish is named after a character or title from the series. How about some hot Hidden Staircase Biscuits or Crossword Cipher Chicken? Typically, given her tendency to overindulge in sweets, Bess Marvin is featured on page 46 with Bess's Secret Chocolate Waffles.

Even Nancy's pet is in on the action with Togo Dogs. Recipes are provided for a variety of meals for breakfast, lunch, and dinner, and for special events like picnics. Another section deals with international dishes, including Hong Kong Fortune Cookies and Greek Baklava. The first printing of the book can

The Mystery of the Missing Volume of Larkspur Lane

A truly special find would be the edition of Password to Larkspur Lane that was allegedly released during the summer of 1932 as Nancy Drew volume #9. It was quickly withdrawn from the printing presses and The Sign of the Twisted Candles replaced it as the new volume #9. Larkspur Lane reappeared in September 1933 as volume #10, in a different format.

To date, no Drew collectors have reported that they own a copy of the first 1932 printing of Larkspur Lane.

However, according to series-book specialists David Farah and Geoffrey S. Lapin, there is substantial proof that the volume does exist. The strongest evidence to support this is the appearance of the phrase "Second Printing, September, 1933" on the copyright page of volume #10 of Larkspur Lane. Directly above this it reads: "First Printing, August, 1932." If there had been no first printing in 1932, Grosset & Dunlap wouldn't have mentioned it. If you find the "missing" copy of Password to Larkspur Lane designated as volume #9, or with the sole date of 1932 printed on the copyright page, it could be worth $500 or more.

The first edition of Larkspur Lane released as volume #10 is also a coveted collectible. It is easy to identify because it is one of the only Drew texts that actually says "First Printing" and "Second Printing" on the copyright page. It also lists "Copyright 1932, 1933" and the words "Revised and Enlarged Edition."
Current Value: First printing, volume #10, Password to Larkspur Lane, with dust jacket, © 1932, 1933, Grosset & Dunlap: $125; without dust jacket, in medium blue hardcover with orange lettering on cover: $85.

be identified by the copyright page, where the date "1973" appears. Subsequent printings include both the 1973 date and a phrase such as "1975 Printing."

Current value: First printing, fine condition: $20 to $25; later editions: $10 to $15.

Nancy Drew Cameo Editions

In 1959 and 1960, Grosset & Dunlap issued two sets of six specially bound Nancy Drew Mystery Stories in limited quantities. These are called the Cameo Editions because a picture of a cameo pendant on a turquoise ribbon appears on the endpapers. They are taller than the average Nancy Drew volumes and have color dust jackets illustrated by Polly Bolian. Nine interior black-and-white illustrations are also included.

Current value: With dust jackets in fine condition: $25 to $35 each book; books without dust jackets: $5 to $10 each book.

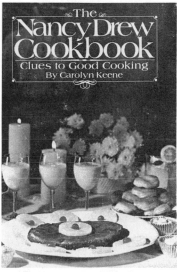

The Nancy Drew Cookbook was published in 1973. (Simon & Schuster)

The Nancy Drew Triple Edition

In the late 1960s, Grosset & Dunlap published the first triple edition Nancy Drew book. It is a thick volume that includes the revised, 1959 versions of *The Secret of the Old Clock*, *The Hidden Staircase*, and *The Bungalow Mystery*. The cover reads: "Meet . . . NANCY DREW in these 3 Exciting Mystery Stories." One edition, released around 1972, has a yellow picture-cover (no dust jacket) designed by Rudy Nappi showing Nancy Drew's face surrounded by a clock, a staircase, and a bungalow. The back cover lists Nancy Drew volumes #1 through #49, from *Old Clock* to *The Secret of Mirror Bay*. The endpapers include fifteen line drawings from various Drew mysteries.

Current value: $10 to $15.

Nancy Drew and the Hardy Boys

This is a paperback book produced by Peggy Herz for Scholastic Books in conjunction with the Nancy Drew television series. It features the history of the Nancy Drew series along with behind-the-scenes information and stills from the TV show. The initial printings had Pamela Sue Martin on the cover.

This Nancy Drew cameo was designed by Polly Bolian. (Simon & Schuster)

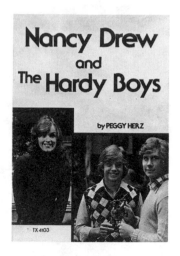

The first edition of Scholastic's *Nancy Drew and the Hardy Boys* had Pamela Sue Martin on the cover. (Scholastic, Inc.)

Later versions picture Janet Louise Johnson, Martin's replacement. The copyright date is 1977; published by Scholastic Magazines, 76 pages.

Current value: $5 to $8.

Nancy Drew Boxed Gift Sets

A number of boxed sets were issued over the years. One, released by Simon & Schuster in the early 1980s, includes paperback editions of volumes #56, #57, and #58 in a box featuring the cover art from *The Triple Hoax*. The box reads: "Includes Three of the Newest Mysteries."

Current value: $15 to $20 complete.

The Hardy Boys and Nancy Drew Meet Dracula

Probably one of the oddest character combinations in Nancy Drew history, *The Hardy Boys and Nancy Drew Meet Dracula* was released by Grosset & Dunlap in conjunction with the television series in 1978. It is an adaptation of the first two episodes of the second season of the show. Issued in softcover for $3.95 (103 pages), it features photos from the episodes. A similar title, *Nancy Drew/Hardy Boys in Transylvania*, was issued in 1979.

Current value: $8 to $10.

Coloring Books

A number of coloring books were published under Grosset & Dunlap's Treasure Books Label, including *Nancy Drew Mystery Pictures to Color* and *Nancy Drew Clues to Color* (both 1977). The cover art was done by Rudy Nappi, with interior designs by Tony Tallarico. The line drawings were adapted from illustrations in the Nancy Drew Mystery Stories. First printings originally sold for $1 and were published in 8½" X 11" softcover format.

Current value: $2 to $5.

Activity Books

The Nancy Drew Mystery Activity Books, versions 1, 2, and 3, were released by Grosset & Dunlap in 1977 under the Elephant Books

Nancy Drew investigates a cemetery in this illustration from *Nancy Drew Mystery Pictures to Color* #1. (Simon & Schuster)

label. They measure 8½" ✗ 11" and were issued in softcover. At one point they were issued as a boxed set.

   Current value: Books alone: $2 to $5; with box: $15.

Puzzle Books

These paperbacks, measuring 5" ✗ 8 ¼," feature still photos and trivia from the Hardy Boys/Nancy Drew television show interspersed with educational material. The activities and puzzles in the books incorporate Nancy Drew plots and characters. The original price of the books ranged from $1.00 to $1.50. Although endearing to review, collectible buyers prefer that the answers are not filled in by previous owners!

These books, copyright 1977 and published by Grosset & Dunlap/Tempo label, included:

Nancy Drew Mystery Mazes by Vladimir Kaziakin
Nancy Drew Secret Codes by Evan Morley
Nancy Drew, Detective Logic Puzzles by Wayne Williams
Nancy Drew Secret Scrambled Word Finds by Linda Doherty
Nancy Drew Clever Crosswords by Dawn Gerber

Current value: $2 to $6 each.

Picture Books for Early Readers

Geared to the younger set, two picture books were released by Grosset & Dunlap in 1977: *A Picture Book Nancy Drew: The Mystery of the Lost Dogs* and *A Picture Book Nancy Drew: The Secret of the Twin Puppets.* Both are oversized hardcovers, 62 pages each.

Current value: $7 to $10 each.

Foreign Editions

During the 1950s, Nancy Drew started to gain marked popularity in numerous countries. Recently, many of these editions have become available to American collectors. These volumes, which were issued in a variety of cover designs and formats, vary widely in value.

Through the decades, numerous magazine articles have reported that the Nancy Drew Mystery Stories were translated into fourteen languages; others cited numbers as high as twenty-five. Because the foreign publishing market ebbs and flows, there are no accurate statistics of exactly how many different countries have licensed and translated the Nancy Drew mysteries since the 1930s. The Nancy Drew Files and other select titles are also being translated, adding to the confusion.

For example, although Nancy was selling well in Italy during the 1960s, according to Simon & Schuster the series is no longer distributed there. On the other hand, the company recently licensed rights to Poland and Lithuania, two countries where the character of Nancy was previously considered unacceptable.

Nancy often undergoes a name change when she travels

Opposite page: The international editions of Nancy Drew mysteries, which have been issued in more than seventeen different countries, are popular text collectibles with current values between $10 and $20. Those pictured here were released in the British Commonwealth, Israel, Italy, and France, where Nancy was renamed "Alice Roy."

ALICE
et le clavecin

CAROLINE QUINE

BIBLIOTHEQUE VERTE

Carolyn Keene

La diligenza
della paura

SERIE NANCY DREW
IL GIALLO DEI RAGAZZI

ARNOLDO MONDADORI EDITORE

THE NANCY DREW SERIES
The Secret in the
Old Attic

CAROLYN KEENE

60

קרולין קין

תעלומת
האורלוגין

overseas. In Sweden Nancy is known as "Kitty," in Finland she is "Nerte," and in France she is called "Alice Roy." The French series lists the author as "Caroline Quine," and Nancy's housekeeper Hannah Gruen is known as "Sarah." Reportedly "Nancy" was not considered a proper name for a French girl sleuth and Alice was the preferred alternative; in upcoming years, however, the French girl sleuth may indeed appear under her true birthname, Nancy.

Overseas publishers prefer Nancy as a redhead. Most of the foreign covers pictured on page 161 feature Nancy with strawberry blonde or titian hair. The Italian Nancy even has freckles!

When collectors find foreign editions of the original Nancy Drew Mystery Stories, they often try to figure out the titles of the books themselves before seeking out a translator. Figuring out the mystery is fun!

Can you match the French Nancy Drew mystery to the American name for that same book?

1. Alice et LE MÉDAILLON D'OR.   a. The Clue of the Broken Locket

2. Alice et LE CHANDELIER   b. The Mystery of the Ivory Charm

3. Alice et L'AVION FANTÔME   c. The Sign of the Twisted Candles

4. Alice et LE TALISMAN D'IVOIRE   d. The Sky Phantom

Answers: 1,a; 2,c; 3,d; 4,b.

Current value: Foreign hardcover editions of Nancy Drew Mystery Stories are priced between $10 and $12, with paperback versions ranging from $3 to $8.

Collectible Games, Dolls, and Educational Aides

There is nothing quite as thrilling for Nancy Drew collectors as unexpectedly stumbling upon a game, lunch box, or other item at a secluded country thrift shop or a neighbor's yard sale. To former owners, these items are simply junk cluttering up the basement, but to Drew fans they're gold! Many special items have been released in conjunction with the series since the late 1950s. What follows is a sampling of the most popular. Remember, prices represent only *approximate* values.

This puzzle, from the private collection of John Van Meter, reads "Nancy Drew Mystery Jigsaw Puzzle—Casse Tête." (Photo by Joe Lance)

The Nancy Drew Jigsaw Puzzle

In 1978 American Publishing Company issued a 121-piece Nancy Drew Mystery Jigsaw Puzzle. It pictures Nancy backing down a staircase toward a landing. A dog and a club-wielding ogre complete the scene. The puzzle picture appears on the box.

Current value: $15 to $30 complete.

The Nancy Drew Halloween Costume

In 1977 a Nancy Drew costume was produced by Collegeville Costumes of Pennsylvania. It features a simple, short-sleeved red dress with black and white trim and the words "Nancy Drew" written across the front of the garment. The costume came in a box, complete with plastic face mask. A tag on the costume also says: Universal City Studios, 1978, Universal City, California.

Current value: $20 to $30.

Nancy Drew Book and Record Sets

Produced by KidStuff Records & Tapes of Florida, the Nancy Drew read-along book and record set was designed for ages four and up, and issued in at least three versions. It includes one 45-rpm record and a fourteen-page fully illustrated storybook. The stories include *The Sea Monster Mystery*, *The Secret of the Vanishing Pyramid*, and *The Case of the Whispering Ghost*.

Current value: $10 to $15 complete.

The Madame Alexander Nancy Drew doll appeared in 1967. (Photo by Joe Lance)

The Nancy Drew Doll

The only doll ever based on Nancy Drew was designed without the Stratemeyer Syndicate's approval and therefore had a short shelf life. In 1967 award-winning doll company Madame Alexander introduced "Nancy Drew," priced at $10.99. Made of plastic vinyl and measuring approximately twelve inches tall, the doll came in a box, packed in tissue paper. "Nancy" was released in two styles. In version #1262, the sleuth sports a dress and a long plaid coat; in #1264 she wears a dress and short jacket—both versions available with pink or blue clothes. The dolls also feature nylon stockings, white boots, a red purse, a camera, sunglasses, and a hair ribbon. (Some dolls also have a pair of binoculars.) Nancy's hair is red-brown. A clothing tag reads "Nancy Drew," and a wrist tag states "I am Nancy Drew."

The Nancy Drew doll has an intriguing history. According to *Farah's Price Guide*, Harriet S. Adams was quoted in the *Chicago Tribune* as late as 1977 stating that there was never a Nancy Drew doll on the market. Adams admitted there "almost was," but because it looked too babyish, the syndicate didn't approve of it and the doll was never manufactured. Despite these statements, a doll bearing Nancy's name did reach the public.

Why a doll was never designed or endorsed by the ever-industrious Stratemeyer Syndicate is mystery in itself, because Mrs. Adams was a serious collector: she owned at least two thousand dolls. The Madame Alexander Nancy Drew doll is extremely rare and highly prized among collectors.

Current value: $250 to $500.

The Nancy Drew Mysteries Lunch Box

This metal lunch box, issued in 1977, is red with a white plastic handle and three-piece thermos. It was manufactured and distributed by Thermos Division, King-Seeley Thermos Co., ©1977 Universal Studios. The box pictures Nancy, Ned, and George in various poses. Nancy resembles Pamela Sue Martin, and Ned Nickerson is shown wearing glasses, just like George O'Hanlon's "Ned" in the television show. A Hardy Boys version was also introduced, picturing the TV series' stars Shaun Cassidy and Parker Stevenson.

Current value: $20 to $30 complete.

My Nancy Drew Date Book and Homework Planner

In 1980 Simon & Schuster issued this planner, available in two styles and designed to fit into a three-ring binder.

Current value: $10 to $15.

The Nancy Drew Private Eye Diary

In 1979 Simon & Schuster issued a 416-page hardcover diary designed to hold private thoughts, names and addresses, important dates, and other information. The first edition has a white cover and was originally priced at $6. The second version has a red cover, priced at $6.95. Both editions came with a lock

These Nancy Drew and Hardy Boys lunch boxes were TV series tie-ins. (Photo by Joe Lance)

and key. The diary was the first spin-off product released directly by Simon & Schuster.

Current value: White (first issue), $20 to $25; red, $10 to $12.

Nancy Drew/Hardy Boys Greeting Card Kit

Issued in 1978 by Cartoonarama, this kit included paint jars, a brush, cards, envelopes, instructions, and more to make custom greeting cards. The box states "Cartoonarama Presents Hardy Boys/Nancy Drew."

Current value: $25 to $30 complete.

The Nancy Drew Mystery Game

Parker Brothers produced two editions of the Nancy Drew Mystery Game, but the only major difference between the 1957 and 1959 versions is the cover design on the box. The first version features Nancy dressed in a red raincoat and cap, her flashlight shining on a house atop a hill. The second shows the sleuth in a green raincoat (no cap), peering from behind a wall. Both scenes depict a thunderstorm. The game is marked with the Stratemeyer Syndicate copyright.

The basic object of the game is to find Nancy and determine which case she is working on. The first player to do so is the winner.

Parker Brothers produced the Nancy Drew Mystery Game in 1957. This box shows Nancy in a red raincoat and hat. A second version showed Nancy in a green coat without a hat. (Photo by Joe Lance)

If you locate a game intact, you will see a game board, four car tokens, four sets of colored markers, dice, forty mystery cards, and an advertising flyer for other Parker Brothers games, including Monopoly.

The game board itself is worthy of framing: it shows a variety of full-color miniscenes from Nancy's cases, including *The Secret of Red Gate Farm*, *The Message in the Hollow Oak*, and *The Secret in the Old Attic*. In the middle of the game board are two square areas for placing the mystery cards and "discards." The board also shows a menacing spider web and a haunted bridge!

Parker Brothers also issued a Hardy Boys mystery game in 1957. That year, the Hardys had two serials running on the Mickey Mouse Club, and Nancy and her male counterparts were enjoying resurgent success among youngsters.

The Nancy Drew game commands a wide range of prices. Because of the game's scarcity, the board alone, even without the playing pieces, is considered a respectable find.

Current value: $40 to $75 complete.

As mentioned earlier, other nonbook collectibles include lobby cards from the Nancy Drew movies of the 1930s, stills and autographed publicity shots featuring the stars from the television show, and programs from Nancy Drew stage productions.

Rarer finds include the original artwork of Nancy Drew cover artists, preliminary line sketches, and business correspondence to and from the Stratemeyer Syndicate.

In the next section you will find a custom-designed grid for keeping track of your Nancy Drew text collectibles.

Your Collection of Nancy Drew Books and Collectibles

COLLECTOR'S NAME:

_____

Directions: This is designed to help you track your Nancy Drew books and collectibles. The first section lists the original fifty-six Nancy Drew Mystery Stories, published by Grosset & Dunlap. Sections two and three list the "new collectibles," Nancy Drew Mystery Stories dated 1979 to 1991, produced in paperback by Simon & Schuster, and the Nancy Drew Files, Cases #1 to #79. Section four is a blank grid for you to list Nancy Drew special editions and memorabilia such as the game and doll.

Beside each volume title and copyright date you will see the heading "Description." In this column you can make personal notes concerning the type of book (e.g., is it a blue or yellow cover?), the condition of the book, and information about the type of endpapers used in that printing. The column labeled "Cost/Buying Guide" is for you to record the amount you paid for the book and the date and place where you purchased it.

In section one below, you will see that there are two listings for many titles. The earliest date represents the original text version; the second (later) date indicates the revised text version. It is important to understand that the actual name of some books changed slightly over the years. For example, volume #29 was called *The Mystery at the Ski Jump* in the 1952 edition, but was changed to simply *Mystery at the Ski Jump* in 1968. Happy collecting!

Volumes #1 to #56, published in hardcover by Grosset & Dunlap.

VOLUME	COPY-RIGHT DATE	TITLE	DESCRIPTION	DUST JACKET? NO	YES	COST/ BUYING GUIDE
#1	1930	The Secret of the Old Clock	_____	___	___	_____
#1	1959	The Secret of the Old Clock	_____	___	___	_____
#2	1930	The Hidden Staircase	_____	___	___	_____
#2	1959	The Hidden Staircase	_____	___	___	_____
#3	1930	The Bungalow Mystery	_____	___	___	_____
#3	1960	The Bungalow Mystery	_____	___	___	_____
#4	1930	The Mystery at Lilac Inn	_____	___	___	_____
#4	1961	The Mystery at Lilac Inn	_____	___	___	_____
#5	1931	The Secret at Shadow Ranch	_____	___	___	_____
#5	1965	The Secret of Shadow Ranch	_____	___	___	_____
#6	1931	The Secret of Red Gate Farm	_____	___	___	_____
#6	1961	The Secret of Red Gate Farm	_____	___	___	_____
#7	1932	The Clue in the Diary	_____	___	___	_____
#7	1962	The Clue in the Diary	_____	___	___	_____
#8	1932	Nancy's Mysterious Letter	_____	___	___	_____
#8	1968	Nancy's Mysterious Letter	_____	___	___	_____
#9	1933	The Sign of the Twisted Candles	_____	___	___	_____
#9	1968	The Sign of the Twisted Candles	_____	___	___	_____
#10	1933	The Password to Larkspur Lane	_____	___	___	_____
#10	1966	Password to Larkspur Lane	_____	___	___	_____
#11	1934	The Clue of the Broken Locket	_____	___	___	_____
#11	1965	The Clue of the Broken Locket	_____	___	___	_____
#12	1935	The Message in the Hollow Oak	_____	___	___	_____
#12	1972	The Message in the Hollow Oak	_____	___	___	_____
#13	1936	The Mystery of the Ivory Charm	_____	___	___	_____
#13	1974	The Mystery of the Ivory Charm	_____	___	___	_____
#14	1937	The Whispering Statue	_____	___	___	_____
#14	1970	The Whispering Statue	_____	___	___	_____
#15	1937	The Haunted Bridge	_____	___	___	_____
#15	1972	The Haunted Bridge	_____	___	___	_____
#16	1939	The Clue of the Tapping Heels	_____	___	___	_____
#16	1969	The Clue of the Tapping Heels	_____	___	___	_____
#17	1940	The Mystery of the Brass Bound Trunk	_____	___	___	_____
#17	1976	Mystery of the Brass-Bound Trunk	_____	___	___	_____
#18	1941	The Mystery at the Moss-Covered Mansion	_____	___	___	_____
#18	1971	The Mystery of the Moss-Covered Mansion	_____	___	___	_____
#19	1942	The Quest of the Missing Map	_____	___	___	_____

VOLUME	COPY-RIGHT DATE	TITLE	DESCRIPTION	DUST JACKET? NO	YES	COST/ BUYING GUIDE
#19	1969	The Quest of the Missing Map				
#20	1943	The Clue in the Jewel Box				
#20	1972	The Clue in the Jewel Box				
#21	1944	The Secret in the Old Attic				
#21	1970	The Secret in the Old Attic				
#22	1945	The Clue in the Crumbling Wall				
#22	1973	The Clue in the Crumbling Wall				
#23	1946	The Mystery of the Tolling Bell				
#23	1973	The Mystery of the Tolling Bell				
#24	1947	The Clue in the Old Album				
#24	1977	The Clue in the Old Album				
#25	1948	The Ghost of Blackwood Hall				
#25	1967	The Ghost of Blackwood Hall				
#26	1949	The Clue of the Leaning Chimney				
#26	1967	The Clue of the Leaning Chimney				
#27	1950	The Secret of the Wooden Lady				
#27	1967	The Secret of the Wooden Lady				
#28	1951	The Clue of the Black Keys				
#28	1968	The Clue of the Black Keys				
#29	1952	The Mystery at the Ski Jump				
#29	1968	Mystery at the Ski Jump				
#30	1953	The Clue of the Velvet Mask				
#30	1969	Clue of the Velvet Mask				
#31	1953	The Ringmaster's Secret				
#31	1974	The Ringmaster's Secret				
#32	1954	The Scarlet Slipper Mystery				
#32	1974	The Scarlet Slipper Mystery				
#33	1955	The Witch Tree Symbol				
#33	1975	The Witch Tree Symbol				
#34	1956	The Hidden Window Mystery				
#34	1975	The Hidden Window Mystery				
#35	1957	The Haunted Showboat				
#36	1959	The Secret of the Golden Pavilion				
#37	1960	The Clue in the Old Stagecoach				
#38	1961	The Mystery of the Fire Dragon				

Volume #38 was the last book issued in blue hardcover with dust jacket. Volumes #39 through #56 were yellow picture-cover hardcovers.

#39	1962	The Clue of the Dancing Puppet				
#40	1963	The Moonstone Castle Mystery				
#41	1964	The Clue of the Whistling Bagpipes				
#42	1965	The Phantom of Pine Hill				
#43	1966	The Mystery of the 99 Steps				
#44	1967	The Clue in the Crossword Cipher				

VOLUME	COPY-RIGHT DATE	TITLE	DESCRIPTION	DUST JACKET? NO	YES	COST/ BUYING GUIDE
#45	1968	The Spider Sapphire Mystery	_____	___	___	_____
#46	1969	The Invisible Intruder	_____	___	___	_____
#47	1970	The Mysterious Mannequin	_____	___	___	_____
#48	1971	The Crooked Banister	_____	___	___	_____
#49	1972	The Secret of Mirror Bay	_____	___	___	_____
#50	1973	The Double Jinx Mystery	_____	___	___	_____
#51	1974	Mystery of the Glowing Eye	_____	___	___	_____
#52	1975	The Secret of the Forgotten City	_____	___	___	_____
#53	1976	The Sky Phantom	_____	___	___	_____
#54	1977	Strange Message in the Parchment	_____	___	___	_____
#55	1978	Mystery of Crocodile Island	_____	___	___	_____
#56	1979	The Thirteenth Pearl	_____	___	___	_____

Section Two: The New Paperback Nancy Drew Mystery Stories

Produced by Simon & Schuster in paperback since 1979, released with picture covers (no dust jackets) under the Minstrel, and later the Wanderer, imprints.

VOLUME	COPY-RIGHT DATE	TITLE	DESCRIPTION	DUST JACKET? NO	YES	COST/ BUYING GUIDE
#57	1979	The Triple Hoax	_____	___	___	_____
#58	1980	The Flying Saucer Mystery	_____	___	___	_____
#59	1980	The Secret in the Old Lace	_____	___	___	_____
#60	1980	The Greek Symbol Mystery	_____	___	___	_____
#61	1981	The Swami's Ring	_____	___	___	_____
#62	1981	The Kachina Doll Mystery	_____	___	___	_____
#63	1981	The Twin Dilemma	_____	___	___	_____
#64	1981	Captive Witness	_____	___	___	_____
#65	1982	Mystery of the Winged Lion	_____	___	___	_____
#66	1982	Race Against Time	_____	___	___	_____
#67	1982	The Sinister Omen	_____	___	___	_____
#68	1982	The Elusive Heiress	_____	___	___	_____
#69	1982	Clue in the Ancient Disguise	_____	___	___	_____
#70	1983	The Broken Anchor	_____	___	___	_____
#71	1983	The Silver Cobweb	_____	___	___	_____
#72	1983	The Haunted Carousel	_____	___	___	_____
#73	1984	Enemy Match	_____	___	___	_____
#74	1984	The Mysterious Image	_____	___	___	_____
#75	1984	The Emerald-Eyed Cat Mystery	_____	___	___	_____

VOLUME	COPY-RIGHT DATE	TITLE	DESCRIPTION	DUST JACKET? NO	DUST JACKET? YES	COST/ BUYING GUIDE
#76	1985	The Eskimo's Secret				
#77	1985	The Bluebeard Room				
#78	1985	The Phantom of Venice				
#79	1987	The Double Horror of Fenley Place				
#80	1987	The Case of the Disappearing Diamonds				
#81	1988	The Mardi Gras Mystery				
#82	1988	The Clue in the Camera				
#83	1988	The Case of the Vanishing Veil				
#84	1988	The Joker's Revenge				
#85	1988	The Secret of the Shady Glen				
#86	1988	The Mystery of Misty Canyon				
#87	1988	The Case of the Rising Stars				
#88	1988	The Search for Cindy Austin				
#89	1989	The Case of the Disappearing Deejay				
#90	1989	The Puzzle at Pineview School				
#91	1989	The Girl Who Couldn't Remember				
#92	1989	The Ghost of Craven Cove				
#93	1990	The Case of the Safecracker's Secret				
#94	1990	The Picture-Perfect Mystery				
#95	1990	The Silent Suspect				
#96	1990	The Case of the Photo Finish				
#97	1990	The Mystery at Magnolia Mansion				
#98	1990	The Haunting of Horse Island				
#99	1991	The Secret of Seven Rocks				
#100	1991	A Secret in Time: Nancy Drew's 100th Anniversary Edition				
#101	1991	The Mystery of the Missing Millionairess				
#102	1991	A Secret in the Dark				
#103	1991	The Stranger in the Shadows				
#104	1991	The Mystery of the Jade Tiger				
#105	1992	The Clue in the Antique Trunk				
#106	1992	The Case of the Artful Crime				
#107	1992	The Legend of Miner's Creek				
#108	1992	The Secret of the Tibetan Treasure				
#109	1992	The Mystery of the Masked Rider				
#110	1992	The Nutcracker Ballet Mystery				

Issued by Simon & Schuster in paperback under the Pocket/Archway imprint.

VOLUME	COPY-RIGHT DATE	TITLE	DESCRIPTION	DUST JACKET? NO	YES	COST/ BUYING GUIDE
#1	1986	Secrets Can Kill				
#2	1986	Deadly Intent				
#3	1986	Murder on Ice				
#4	1986	Smile and Say Murder				
#5	1986	Hit and Run Holiday				
#6	1986	White Water Terror				
#7	1987	Deadly Doubles				
#8	1987	Two Points for Murder				
#9	1987	False Moves				
#10	1987	Buried Secrets				
#11	1987	Heart of Danger				
#12	1987	Fatal Ransom				
#13	1987	Wings of Fear				
#14	1987	This Side of Evil				
#15	1987	Trial by Fire				
#16	1987	Never Say Die				
#17	1987	Stay Tuned for Danger				
#18	1987	Circle of Evil				
#19	1988	Sisters in Crime				
#20	1988	Very Deadly Yours				
#21	1988	Recipe for Murder				
#22	1988	Fatal Attraction				
#23	1988	Sinister Paradise				
#24	1988	Till Death Do Us Part				
#25	1988	Rich and Dangerous				
#26	1988	Playing with Fire				
#27	1988	Most Likely to Die				
#28	1988	The Black Widow				
#29	1988	Pure Poison				
#30	1988	Death by Design				
#31	1989	Trouble in Tahiti				
#32	1989	High Marks for Malice				
#33	1989	Danger in Disguise				
#34	1989	Vanishing Act				
#35	1989	Bad Medicine				
#36	1989	Over the Edge				
#37	1989	Last Dance				
#38	1989	The Final Scene				

VOLUME	COPY-RIGHT DATE	TITLE	DESCRIPTION	DUST JACKET? NO	YES	COST/ BUYING GUIDE
#39	1989	The Suspect Next Door				
#40	1989	Shadow of a Doubt				
#41	1989	Something to Hide				
#42	1989	The Wrong Chemistry				
#43	1990	False Impressions				
#44	1990	Scent of Danger				
#45	1990	Out of Bounds				
#46	1990	Win, Place or Die				
#47	1990	Flirting with Danger				
#48	1990	A Date with Deception (A Summer Love Trilogy #1)				
#49	1990	Portrait in Crime (A Summer Love Trilogy #2)				
#50	1990	Deep Secrets (A Summer Love Trilogy #3)				
#51	1990	A Model Crime				
#52	1990	Danger for Hire				
#53	1990	Trail of Lies				
#54	1990	Cold as Ice				
#55	1991	Don't Look Twice				
#56	1991	Make No Mistake				
#57	1991	Into Thin Air				
#58	1991	Hot Pursuit				
#59	1991	High Risk				
#60	1991	Poison Pen				
#61	1991	Sweet Revenge				
#62	1991	Easy Marks				
#63	1991	Mixed Signals				
#64	1991	The Wrong Track				
#65	1991	Final Notes				
#66	1992	Tall, Dark and Deadly				
#67	1992	Nobody's Business				
#68	1992	Crosscurrents				
#69	1992	Running Scared				
#70	1992	Cutting Edge				
#71	1992	Hot Tracks				
#72	1992	Swiss Secrets				
#73	1992	Rendezvous in Rome				
#74	1992	Greek Odyssey				
#75	1992	A Talent for Murder				
#76	1992	The Perfect Plot				
#77	1992	Danger on Parade				
#78	1992	Update on Crime				
#79	1993	No Laughing Matter				

Section Four: My Record of Nancy Drew Collectibles and Special Book Editions

NAME OF ITEM   DESCRIPTION AND CONDITION OF COLLECTIBLE

Select Bibliography

This bibliography is by no means a complete record of all the works and sources consulted while writing this book. It indicates the substance and range of reading upon which I have formed my ideas, and I intend it to serve as a convenience for those who wish to pursue further study of the character of Nancy Drew, her creator, the Stratemeyer Syndicate, or historical trends and milestones of the series.

Books

Billman, Carol. *The Secrets of the Stratemeyer Syndicate: Nancy Drew, the Hardy Boys, and the Million Dollar Fiction Factory.* New York: Ungar, 1986.

Caprio, Betsy. *The Mystery of Nancy Drew: Girl Sleuth on the Couch.* Trabuco Canyon, Calif.: Source Books, 1992.

Castleman, Harry, and Walter J. Podrazik. *Harry and Wally's Favorite TV Shows.* Englewood Cliffs, N.J.: Prentice Hall Press, 1989.

Craig, Patricia, and Mary Cadogan. *The Lady Investigates: Women Detectives & Spies in Fiction.* New York: St. Martin's Press, 1981.

Dizer, John T., Jr. *Tom Swift and Company: Boys' Books by Stratemeyer and Others.* Jefferson, N.C.: McFarland, 1982.

Farah, David. *Farah's Price Guide to Nancy Drew Books and Collectibles.* Newport Beach, Calif.: Farah's Books, 1990.

Herz, Peggy. *Nancy Drew and the Hardy Boys.* New York: Scholastic Book Services, 1977.

Johnson, Deidre. *Stratemeyer Pseudonyms and Series Books: An Annotated Checklist of Stratemeyer and Stratemeyer Syndicate Publications.* Westport, Conn.: Greenwood Press, 1982.

Lapin, Geoffrey S. "The Ghost of Nancy Drew." In *Library Lit. 20—: The Best of 1989,* edited by Jane Anne Hannigan. Metuchen, N.J.: The Scarecrow Press, 1990.

McFarlane, Leslie. *The Ghost of the Hardy Boys.* New York: Methuen Press, 1976.

Olendorf, Donna, ed. "Benson, Mildred." In *Something About the Author.* Vol. 65: 7–11. Detroit: Gale Research, 1991.

Penzler, Otto, ed. *The Great Detectives.* Topanga, Calif.: Boulevard Books, 1978.

Pringle, David. *Imaginary People: A Who's Who of Modern Fictional Characters.* New York: Pharos Books, 1988.

Singleton, Linda Joy. "A Brief History of the Genre." In *How to Write a Novel for Young Readers,* edited by Kathryn Falk and Cindy Savage. Fiction Writer's Magazette Series 2, 1990. 18–23.

Articles

Adams, Harriet. "Their Success Is No Mystery." *TV Guide* (15 June 1977): 13–16.

Benson, Mildred Wirt. "More News on Nancy." *Publishers Weekly* (26 September 1986): 12.

Chapman, Bernadine, and Mary Ellen Johnson. "Nancy Drew Collectibles." *The Antiques Journal* (May 1985): 46–48.

Felder, Deborah. "Nancy Drew: Then and Now." *Publishers Weekly* (30 May 1986): 31–32.

Fitzgerald, Frances. "Woman, Success, and Nancy Drew." *Vogue* (May 1980): 323–24.

"For It Was Indeed He." *Fortune* (April 1934):86–89.

Furtak, Joanne. "Of Clues, Kisses, and Childhood Memories: Nancy Drew Revisited." *Seventeen* (May 1984): 90.

Galvin, Helen. "Collecting Nancy Drew." *Firsts* (December 1991): 25–29.

Gates, David. "Nancy Drew: The Eternal Teenager." *Newsweek* (26 March 1984): 12.

Greco, Gail. "Nancy Drew's New Look." *Americana* 14 (September/October, 1986): 57–58.

Grossman, Anita Susan. "The Ghost of Nancy Drew." *Ohio Magazine* (December 1987): 41–43.

Jackson, Gregory, Jr. "Spaceman's Pluck! An Interview with Frankie Thomas." *Yellowback Library* (November/December 1987): 5–14.

Jones, James P. "Nancy Drew: WASP Supergirl of the 1930s." *The Journal of Popular Culture* 6(1973): 707–17.

———. "Negro Stereotypes in Children's Literature: The Case of Nancy Drew." *The Journal of Negro Education* (Spring 1971): 121–25.

Kelly, Ernie. "An Interview with Rudy Nappi." *Yellowback Library* (July 1991): 5–11.

———. "Inside the Stratemeyer Syndicate: Part I." *Yellowback Library* (October 1988): 5–11.

———. "Inside the Stratemeyer Syndicate: Part II." *Yellowback Library* (December 1988): 5–11.

Klemesrud, Judy. "100 Books—and Not a Hippie in Them." *The New York Times*, 4 April 1968: 52.

Kuskin, Karla. "Nancy Drew and Friends." *New York Times Magazine* (4 May 1975): 20–21.

Lapin, Geoffrey S. "Carolyn Keene, pseud." *Yellowback Library* (March/April 1984): 13–16.

———. "Jim Lawrence and the Stratemeyer Syndicate." *Yellowback Library* (January/February 1986): 15.

"Madame Alexander's Contribution to Dolls in America." *Doll Reader* (December 1990/January 1991): 182.

Murphy, Cullen. "Starting Over." *The Atlantic* (June 1991): 18–22.

"Nancy Drew Is Alive and Well in Books and Now on TV." *People* (14 March 1977).

Nugent, Beth. "To: Harriet Stratemeyer Adams. For: Solving the Case of the Missing Role Model." *Redbook* 154 (April 1980): 44.

Nuhn, Marilyn. "Nancy Drew: An Ageless 50 Years Old." *Hobbies* 86 (March 1981): 104–5.

Peterson, Lisa. "Here Lies History." *Newark Star Ledger*, 22 April 1991: 21, 26.

Reuter, M. "Grosset & Dunlap Sues Simon & Schuster and Stratemeyer Syndicate for $50 Million." *Publishers Weekly* (7 May, 1979): 25, 34.

————. "Stratemeyer and S&S Call Grosset Suit Frivolous." *Publishers Weekly* (14 May 1979): 124, 129.

Soderbergh, Peter A. "The Stratemeyer Strain: Educators and the Juvenile Series Book, 1900–1973." *The Journal of Popular Culture* 7 (1974): 864–72.

Vivelo, Jackie. "The Mystery of Nancy Drew." *Ms.* (November/December 1992): 76–77.

Wagner, Sharon. "Solving the Juvenile Mystery." *Fiction Writer's Monthly* (Fall 1988): 54.

Wartik, Nancy. "Nancy Drew, Yuppie Detective." *Ms.* (September 1986): 29.

Watson, Bruce. "Tom Swift, Nancy Drew and Pals All Had the Same Dad." *Smithsonian* (October 1992): 50–52.

Zimmerman, Dick. "Nancy Drew Grows Up." *Playboy* (July 1978): 97–92, 184.

Dear Nancy Drew® Scrapbook Reader:

In my experiences researching six decades of Nancy Drew and the Stratemeyer Syndicate, I have already accumulated numerous files of information concerning the character of Nancy, her history, collectibles, creators, and special fans. But the process of research does not end simply because the first edition of the Scrapbook has been published!

It is important for me to be aware of readers' comments about the book, to know the parts of the Scrapbook you enjoyed the most or the subject you would like to know more about. I need to continue gathering information that could possibly be used in subsequent editions, or incorporated into related articles about Nancy Drew and other girls' series-book heroines.

Therefore, I invite you to send me your information and comments. If you have a collectible item that is not mentioned in the Scrapbook, feel free to send along a photo and a short summary of how you found it. If you have a particularly interesting or humorous story about how Nancy Drew affected your life, I would be delighted to see that as well. I am particularly interested in receiving any copies of local news or magazine articles on Nancy Drew. I am also in the process of researching Hardy Boys collectibles and am interested in information on those.

Please feel free to write:

Karen Plunkett-Powell
Author, Nancy Drew® Scrapbook
P.O. Box 3128
Sea Bright, New Jersey 07760

Looking forward to your comments, information, and responses!